The Fishing Hole

An Alaska Bear Tale

by

Ron Walden

Alaska True to Life Crime Writer

UglymooseAK@gmail.com

Ugly Moose AK

Paperback ISBN: 978-1-957263-39-7

eBook ISBN: 978-1-957263-40-3

Library of Congress Control Number (LCCN): 2023917494

Copyright by Ron Walden

2023 – First Edition

Manufactured in the United States of America

Dedication

I dedicate this novel to all the professional officers of the Alaska State Troopers and Alaska Wildlife Troopers who give so much of themselves to protect the citizens and wildlife of the great State of Alaska. It's this selfless dedication to duty that allows the rest of us to live there in peace and safety. I thank all of them in memory of my late wife and retired Alaska Fish and Wildlife Officer, Betty L. Walden.

Cover Photography:

Heidi Hanson Photography

Soldotna, Alaska

For more amazing photographs of Alaska Brown and Black Bears in the wild, being bears, Contact Heidi Hanson:

Email:

aksk8@outlook.com

Facebook:

HeidihoAK49photography

Instagram:

heidi_ho_ak49_photography

The Fishing Hole

An Alaska Bear Tale

by

Ron Walden

CHAPTER 1

Sergeant Ted Wilson had been in his office since before six A.M. setting duty assignments for the day and reviewing individual requests that had been left on his desk by the late shift last night. It was now a couple of minutes before eight and he heard someone in the office. It was Lynda Dorn, the office receptionist, opening the office for the day. Wilson carried a handful of papers to her desk and said, "Good morning, Lynda."

"Good morning to you, Sergeant. Are you ready for the day?" she greeted.

"Yes, I am. In fact, I'm leaving the office to go flying. I plan to do an air patrol in the Tustamena and Skilak Lakes area. I should be back in the office by noon. Do you have anything for me this morning?"

"I don't think so, Ted. Are the regular patrol officers out yet?"

"Yes, they both left about an hour ago. One to North Kenai and the other out to Swanson River and Paddle Lake. The salmon haven't started to come up those rivers yet, but the trout fishermen will be working. Time to start checking fishing licenses. I'll have my radio if you have any emergencies. The Lieutenant will be in soon. I'll be flying the Cub today."

"I'll tell him. Have fun!" she said as he turned to get his emergency pack from his office.

The Soldotna Airport is only about three miles from the office, and on this early June morning, the weather was perfect for flying the small, two-seater Piper Cub. This one was painted State Trooper blue and white with large numbers painted on the side of the fuselage. This made it very easy to identify the aircraft.

Wilson did a careful preflight check and visually checked the fuel levels of both wing tanks. He also lifted the cowling and looked inside before checking the oil level in the engine. Everything seemed in order and he closed the engine compartment once again. He kept a small baby food jar in the airplane for taking fuel samples to check for condensation in the fuel tanks. There was none. He untied the tiedown ropes and climbed inside the cabin. He wiggled the stick, moved the rudder pedals and noted he had full range of movement. He opened the side window, which opened from the bottom of the plexiglass, to warn any bystander that he was starting his engine.

While the engine warmed, his headset over his ears, he checked the local wind and weather on the Soldotna frequency. Looking around the area he was ready to taxi for take-off. The wind was from the south, a slight crosswind, but only at five miles per hour. Ted loved flying the little Cub and was looking forward to today's flight.

He leveled off at about 1500 feet and turned south toward the Kasilof river. As he approached the river, he could see sport fishing guides launching their boats loaded with anxious clients ready to fish gathered around the launch operation.

Wilson followed the river upstream to its source, the mighty Tustamena Lake. He followed the left shoreline, past the hunting lodges to the north end of the lake. On the right was Tustamena Glacier, but he was going up the other side toward Emma Lake. He'd seen several moose in the area with new calves. It was an encouraging sight.

Climbing at a steady rate, he flew up and over the cabin on Emma Lake. There was nobody at the lake and the cabin appeared empty. He was still climbing, turning slightly to his right, to follow the stream flowing from this tongue of the ice field. A black bear scurried away into the brush near the stream as the airplane approached. This was the reason he enjoyed being a brown shirt Trooper so very much. He loved the outdoors and felt great satisfaction patrolling the wilds of Alaska.

He turned to the North slightly following the mountains toward the Skilak side of the glacier field. Looking to his left he saw something on the peat moss covered hillside and changed his course to investigate. Dropping low to see what the object was. It looked like it could be a dead moose.

As he circled only a few feet above the ground, he was surprised to see it was actually a dead horse. It appeared to have been killed by a bear and carried to this spot. That was puzzling because of the size of the animal.

This was a very large horse, probably owned by the packer who had a cabin and several horses not far down the slope from here. He circled again and photographed the animal and noted its many injuries. The Sergeant eased back on the stick to gain altitude and widened his circle in an attempt to find the bear.

This low ridge has little vegetation at this altitude. He could see a few caribou lying on the ice of the glacier, keeping cool and free of mosquitoes. As he searched the area, he saw something near the brush line on the lower slope.

It looked like a large Brown Bear and was headed back in this direction. Sergeant Ted Wilson flew higher and in a wider circle to avoid startling the bear. As he circled, he saw this was a gigantic bear. At least a ten-footer, possibly a little more. Ted had never seen a bear this large on the Kenai Peninsula. Circling wide, he aimed his camera and snapped several pictures of the animal.

Reaching for his police radio he called the dispatch center. "Call C-16 and have him contact me on our frequency."

"Will do Sergeant," came the reply.

Moments later his other radio frequency crackled, and a voice asked, "What's up Sarge?"

"Hey, Dwight, I'm flying over the ridge south of Skilak Lake and came across a dead horse. It looks like a bear got it. I'll fly over Bill Dover's cabin and see if he's there. I want you to go up there if he is and deliver this message. Stand by and I'll fly over his cabin."

"Roger that," replied the other Wildlife Trooper.

Minutes later Ted Wilson was circling the cabin with its barn and outbuildings. In the corral at the back of the property was a small band of horses. Someone was grooming one of the animals and waved as he flew past.

"C-16" he called into the radio.

"Go ahead, Sarge."

"It looks like Bill Dover is at his cabin. He's out in the corral with his horses. Take a boat up there and tell him one of his animals has been killed and it looks like a big brown bear got it. It's about three miles up the ridge from his cabin. Also tell him the bear is huge and it's still in the area."

"Got it. Anything else?" asked C-16.

"Just warn him about shooting the bear." Ted knew he didn't need to explain his meaning to Dwight.

Ted flew around the area for another several minutes, keeping an eye on the bear and how he was behaving. The bear seemed intent on returning to his kill to continue his spring meal. Ted viewed the scene from a higher altitude and a wider circle.

Wilson was totally amazed when the huge animal returned to the carcass and took several bites of meat from the belly area before juggling the entire carcass onto his back, half carrying and half dragging it nearly a hundred yards up the ridge to a clump of tall grass, where he proceeded to cover it with grass and peat moss he had scratched up with his huge paws.

Dwight would be another hour or more getting to the upper Skilak Lake boat launch with the Trooper boat he'd need to cross the lake. He decided to continue his patrol, following the face of the Kenai Mountains, crossing the Sterling Highway and patrolling toward the natural gas pipeline twenty miles north and west.

He'd seen several cow moose with new calves as he patrolled and was happy to note it was going to be a good growth rate for local moose herds.

As he neared the pipeline road, he saw several Caribou grazing as they walked along the treeless corridor. There were several new calves in this group also.

He was surprised how few campers were in the area even though it was early in the spring season.

He glanced at his watch and decided it was time to return to the Skilak Lake area to see if Dwight had arrived at the lake. He'd just circled back toward the lake when his radio called his number. "Go ahead, Dwight," he replied.

"Just to let you know, I'm launching the boat right now and should be at Bill Dover's cabin in about a half hour."

"Good, I just turned around at the gas pipeline. I'll head back your way. I'll be returning to the office after that. The bear was still in the area when I left. He moved that big horse carcass up the ridge a short way and began to cover it with moss and grass. Take your shotgun with you and if Bill decides to go up to the carcass, I want you to go with him. I don't want him to get angry and shoot that bear."

Wilson didn't mention the photos he had taken of the giant creature but would show them to Dwight when he returned to the office. Over the lake he saw the small powerboat more than half-way across the wide lake, moving fast over calm water on this sunny June day.

As he crossed over the packers' cabin, he saw the man where he had been before, currying his animals. Dover saw the blue and white super cub and, again, he waved at it before continuing to brush his horse. Ted began to gain altitude and turn to his right to avoid stressing the bear.

He pointed his camera toward the bear and took several pictures of the animal as it attempted to cover the dead animal. Since there was little brush or trees in this area it was about as good as the bear could do to cover his prize. He circled wide two more times and decided to head back to the Soldotna Airport and his office.

After landing and securing the aircraft, Ted Wilson returned to the office to report what he had seen to his boss, Lieutenant Del Costas. His written report would be submitted before he went off duty today.

The LT was busy with a visitor causing Ted to go to his office and begin his report. An hour later Lt. Costas called for him to come to his office.

Ted took his camera with him to show his boss how large this creature really was. He spent nearly an hour with his boss discussing ways to proceed with watching the giant bear. It was decided they wouldn't make the discovery public in order to keep curious, careless campers out of the area. There were very few hikers ever seen in this area. They wanted it to stay that way.

Dwight had not yet returned to the office to report his interaction with Bill Dover. Dover was known as a mild-mannered man, but it was his horse the bear had killed which could have tested the packer's good nature.

The Lieutenant was impressed with the photos of the bear and had Ted forward copies of them to his computer. He returned to report writing. It took him the rest of the afternoon to complete the written report. He was nearly finished when Dwight Morgan returned to the office. He had a broad grin on his face when he tapped on the door frame.

Stepping into the office and taking a seat across the desk from his Sergeant, he chuckled. "That was quite a chore you asked me to do today, Sarge."

Ted stopped writing and listened to his officer.

"How did he take it when you told him about the horse?" asked Ted.

"I thought he was gonna cry. He really loves his animals. They're the only neighbors he has out at his cabin. He wanted to get a rifle and go after the bear immediately, but I talked him out of it. He agreed after I told him you thought it was a record size bear, at least for the Kenai Peninsula. He's agreed to keep his horses close to the corral and watch for the bear to come for another meal."

"I've known Bill for a lot of years, and I really like the guy," noted Wilson.

"He told me he's known you for a long time. He said he thought you were an all-right guy too. I lied for you and agreed with him."

"Ok, Dwight, finish your report and leave a copy for me on the desk. Before you go, I want to show you the pictures I took from the airplane." Ted brought them up on his computer.

"I was circling out at a distance so as not to disturb the big brute. You can see him next to the carcass. He was very big. The horse wasn't a saddle pony. It was a big old pack horse. This bear picked that animal up and wrestled it onto his back to carry it up the ridge several hundred feet where he buried it with moss and grass before I left the area. This guy is impressive."

Dwight looked at the photos and agreed this was an unusual bear. He went to his desk to write the incident report and describe how he managed the notification.

Ted forwarded a copy to Lt. Del Morgan before leaving the office for the day. It was time to go home to his family. His wife JoAnne and daughter Lucy would want to go to the river this evening.

CHAPTER 2

When Ted arrived at his home his wife was in the back yard lighting the bar-b-que grill. His daughter, Lucy, was sitting on the back porch watching. When she spotted her father come to the back yard she jumped up and ran to give him a huge hug while screaming, "Daddy!"

"Hi, sweetheart. Did you have a good day?" he asked.

"Yeah, me and mom went to town to go shopping. I had some ice cream at DQ," she replied.

His wife JoAnne just looked at the pair and smiled while lighting the grill.

Holding the young girl in one arm he reached out to hug his wife. "It sounds like you girls had a good day," he remarked.

"Yes, we did. Spent a lot of money. That always makes us girls happy. How was your day?"

"It was great. I spent the early part of it flying. I saw a giant brown bear on the ridge above Skilak lake. It had killed one of Bill Dover's horses. It had to be the largest bear I have ever seen on the Kenai. Even the airplane didn't seem to bother him" explained Wilson.

"I wish we could have seen that," said JoAnne, while spraying non-stick oil on the grill.

"I really don't want to bring too much attention to that big guy. I think he'll stick around the area for a while and maybe we can fly up there in a couple of days to take a look around."

He turned to his daughter, "What would you like to do after dinner, young lady?"

She paused to think for about a second, then looked at him and grinned, "Go to the beach!" she said in her thirteen-year-old tone of voice.

"How about it, Mom? Can we go after dinner?" he asked his patient wife.

"Let's talk about it after we eat," she said, placing steaks on the grill.

After dinner the trio piled into the truck, drove down the beach road, and found a place to walk on the sandy beach looking for seashells. Lucy ran helter-skelter around the beach looking at every piece of rock, stick and trash in the sand. Ted and JoAnne walked behind her, hand in hand, still in love after all these years. The sun was high in the June sky when they walked back to where he had parked his pickup to return home. It was getting late and he had an early day tomorrow.

Back at home, Lucy was put into bed. The two adults sat on the back deck making small talk. "You sounded excited about that bear you saw today. How come?"

"Oh, JoAnne, he's the largest bear I have ever seen on the Kenai Peninsula. I know he's more than a ten-foot bear. He is by far, the most impressive animal I have ever seen. I saw him put a full-size horse on his back and carry it more than a hundred yards up the ridge and begin to bury it.

This guy is massive. I don't want to advertise his location because some trophy hunter would take him the instant the season opens."

"Well, you know I won't say anything, and I'll caution Lucy about saying anything about it." JoAnne knew the rules of the house.

The following morning Ted Wilson was in his office early. He read the report Dwight Morgan had put on his desk and pondered what he was going to do about it. Bill Dover had told Morgan he wasn't going to go after the bear and promised to keep the giant animal a secret for now. Wilson knew there were many trophy hunters who would give an eye tooth for an animal that large. By this afternoon his staff would return to normal numbers, and he could assign someone to deal with the situation.

This office had many different areas to cover. The largest this time of year was the beginning of salmon fishing season, patrolling trout streams, watching for poachers of both fish and game animals. There was also a commercial fishing industry to be policed. The responsibilities of Fish and Wildlife officers were enormous.

There were two female officers in the detachment. One was a short stocky, perky lady with a great sense of humor, Gayle Portman. He would assign her to patrol the lakes and off-road streams on the South Peninsula.

The other was a tall, serious-minded lady who looked more like a movie star than a policeman. She was Betty Holden. A seasoned officer with several years of field experience. He decided she would be perfect to patrol that area of the Kenai River from Kenai Lake to Skilak Lake as well as the area where he had seen the large bear. She was a savvy officer with many years of experience and had no problem working alone in remote sectors of the Peninsula. Over the years she'd dealt with many problem bears and irate citizens who had lost pets and farm animals to them. Ted was confident she would be up to the task.

It took two more hours to make a list of assignments and disperse the team. When Lynda Dean arrived at her desk Ted walked to her office to ask if she would direct Officer Holden to see him when she arrived for the day.

"Yessir, Sergeant," she replied. A half an hour later the tall redhead stepped into his office.

"You wanted to see me?" she asked.

"Yes, thanks, Betty. I have an assignment for you. I don't want you to advertise it around the detachment. I want you to work the rapids and upper Kenai River from Jim's Landing to the lake and the south side of the lake to the glacier. You'll need to take camping gear, but Bill Dover will let you stay at one of his cabins while working down there. Get that guide friend of yours to give you a ride down the rapids to the lake. Have him send me a voucher for the cost. You'll take that new temp with you for a back-up. Carry a shotgun as well as your duty weapon and be very careful."

Officer Holden stared at the ceiling for a moment, then asked. "This sounds a little strange to me, Sarge. What's this all about?"

"Close the door and we'll talk," he said. She did as she was ordered and sat again in the chair.

"This is important to me, Betty. The license check in the upper river is a cover. I want you to keep an eye on a huge brown bear I saw while patrolling by air yesterday. He's at least ten feet. He's a beauty and I want to protect him if possible. I'm telling you to take no chances. He's big and I saw him pick up a dead work horse to carry it up the ridge more than a hundred yards. I'm worried that if the word gets out there will be a lot of bear hunters out to get him, even though the season is three months away. Take an extra battery for your radio and stay in touch with me on my personal channel. Try to get back to Dover's place each night and don't sleep out on the ground if possible. I'll have someone bring supplies to you at Dover's boat dock. That new kid I'm sending with you is studying to be a bear biologist and, I'm hoping he knows enough to be of help." Ted looked at his officer, "Still want the job?" he asked, smiling.

"How long do you want me to stay up there?" she asked.

"I'm not sure, but I believe he'll want to move on after he consumes all that horse meat. It should take him about four or five days to do that. Unless he comes back for another horse, I think he will move back to the upper Kenai for the early run of Red Salmon that's about to start. If he does that, he's going to be on public display and we can't do anything about that. If he leaves the ridge to return to the river, I expect him to be a problem. Gawkers will be the worst, but he'll be attacking every cub a sow brings to the river. I'm guessing he'll want to fish in the shallows above Jim's landing where those sows usually fish with young cubs. Every year someone shoots one or more of them and claims self-defense. I want to avoid that situation, if possible."

"Sounds like this could be a very long assignment," she noted.

"It could be Betty, but once he becomes a public attraction the gloves will be off. We'll have to play it by ear. I am going to advise Forestry we may call on them in case of an emergency while you're out there." He paused a moment, "Any other questions?" he asked.

"None I can think of right now. Send that new kid to my office to help. What's his name, anyway?"

"Les Goddard. Seems like a nice kid, but green as grass. Make him carry his own weight, but also, try to teach him a little about brown bears. He's only dealt with them in books."

CHAPTER 3

Les Goddard was a personable young man with a sharp sense of humor. He'd spent his entire life on the family farm in northern Iowa. He was a strong young man, having worked on the farm his entire life. The strange thing about this young man was that he had never seen a bear in his entire life. There were no bears of any kind in his part of Iowa.

As a youth, he became fascinated with stories the older folks told while visiting in the evenings. One of his uncles had been stationed in Alaska while in the military and had many tales and adventures to relate during the hot summer evenings. These stories had somehow influenced his decision to become a bear biologist as his chosen career.

Just 21 years old and a junior at the University of Washington, which he had chosen because of the highly rated biology department, he'd participated in several field trips to tag black bears and study their habits. This trip to Alaska would be his first chance to encounter the large species of Brown Bear…the coastal Alaska Grizzly.

It was immediately apparent to Betty Holden that this young man was full of book information, but lacked any first-hand knowledge of the animals he was studying. Her conversation with him led her to believe he was familiar with what the textbooks said about the disposition and personality of a Brown Bear, but he'd never encountered one in person. That was about to change.

Betty called and arranged to meet with the river guide who had agreed to take them down river from Cooper Landing to Skilak Lake. With their gear stowed in the Fish and Wildlife truck driven by the officer assigned to the Russian River area for the day, the two officers rode the hour-long trip with Betty explaining what they were doing on this trip beginning today. At a lodge a half mile below the bridge on the highway through Cooper Landing, they unloaded their gear and said goodbye to the driver.

It was still very early in the morning when they loaded the equipment into the drift boat they would use to float down the river through the rapids above the lake. The small drift boat was unusual in that it had a square end and a small motor attached. This was to aid in crossing the open water of Skilak lake where boat motors were legal.

Bob Corben was a skilled operator and had been a guide on the upper river for many years. Betty had known him as a skillful and honest operator. She knew he'd keep her real mission confidential, though they'd check licenses as they floated down the river above the rapids. Corben gave the pair the mandatory lecture about what to do and what not to do while on board. He assisted

Les in fastening his life vest properly, checked both passengers and pushed off into the current of the upper river.

"Last chance for a cup of coffee, Betty," offered Bob.

"Thanks, but I'm good. How about you Les?" she inquired.

"No thanks, I'm good. I'm just anxious to go to work and to see some bears." Les was filled with enthusiasm and anticipation.

"There's been a sow and two cubs working the shallows below the Russian River. We might get to see 'em this morning, if we're lucky," announced Bob.

"Remember Les, no loud sudden movement or sounds if we see the bears. We don't want to provoke an incident," reminded Betty.
Les nodded in agreement while Betty nodded back.

"OK Bob, once we get past the Russian River area we can stop and check licenses of those folks fishing from the shoreline." Les wore a plaid shirt and jeans, but Betty was in a full brown shirt uniform.

It was a lazy float with many wildlife sightings of river ducks, shore birds and near Juneau Creek, a pair of river otters were playing. A large number of Dall sheep were scattered along the ridges above the river. For Les it was a dream come true. Traveling downriver, and just above the Russian River at a place named Schooner Bend, there was a large, fat, black bear sitting on the upper end of the gravel bar. Not bothering to move as they drifted by, he only looked at the intruders and watched them drift along.

Once around the bend, Les said, "Wow, that was exciting! That was my first real bear sighting."

Betty smiled at the neophyte, "It's alright to take pictures if you want. Just don't let it interfere with our duties."

"Oh, gosh, I never even thought about taking a picture," he said, snickering at himself.

As they neared the place where the ferry used to take fishermen across the Kenai River and the Russian River confluence, Betty announced, "We'll leave this area to the other officers. We'll begin checking around the next set of bends. Just pull in when we see fishermen, Bob."

Around the second bend there were a pair of fishermen on a long gravel shore. Bob eased the drift boat to the beach, attempting not to disturb the fishing spot. Betty and Les walked up the beach to where the men were fishing. "How's fishing, Guys?" she asked.

"A little slow this morning, but it'll pick up after a while. We just like to get our spot early," replied one of the fishermen.

"Have you caught anything this morning?" she asked.

"Not yet, but we did well yesterday," the other replied.

"Do you mind if I trouble you for your fishing licenses?" asked the lady officer.

The first fisherman set his rod on the shore and reached for his license, presenting it to the officer. The other man did the same. Betty checked the documents and thanked them for cooperating. "Good luck, Men," she called as she climbed into the boat.

This process was repeated many times during the float above the rapids, but once inside the narrow canyon where the water began to gain momentum there would be no chance to stop their boat to check the fishermen. There would be few bank fishermen in the canyon.

As the speed of the current began to increase, the ride became more challenging. Bob Corben was an experienced guide and made this trip almost daily. He skillfully maneuvered the drift boat through the white-water rapids down the river for another nearly five miles.

As they reached quieter water exiting the canyon and nearing the lake, Bob became more relaxed and again began to start conversation.

"Too bad you aren't fishing, Les. This stretch is really great. When we get out of the river and into the lake, I'll start the motor and head to Dover's place. Does he know you're coming?"

"Yes," replied Betty, "He's supposed to have a cabin ready for us and be waiting at the dock. When we get out onto the lake, I'll call Ted and have him call Dover on his radio."

Bob nodded his understanding and watched the shoreline as they crossed the river of glacial silt exiting the glacier canyon side of the lake. "Les. Look on the shore below us, there's a nice brown bear and two cubs looking for fish."

As Les began to look, Bob pointed to the spot where the bears were standing near a clump of willows. When Les finally spotted the bears, he became very excited and turned to Betty to be sure she'd also seen them. She only smiled and nodded, confirming she had.

Early season Sockeye Salmon are, as a rule, much smaller in size than the later run fish. There seemed to be a bumper crop of fish heading into the canyon this morning. The bears would have a good day fishing here above Skilak Lake.

As the boat left the river and entered the lake, she took her portable radio from her belt to call Ted Wilson and alert him to their arrival.

The motor propelling the boat was small. Progress was slow but steady. It took more than an hour to reach the boat dock at Dover's lodge. He was waiting for them when they arrived. It took only a few minutes to unload the boat and allow Bob Corben to leave for his pick-up point at the upper Skilak Boat Landing.

As they watched the river guide set out across the lake, Bill Dover greeted his guests, "Good to see you again, Officer Holden," he said as he held out his hand to shake hers.

"Now Bill, you know you've earned the right to call me Betty." She took his hand in both of hers and greeted him. "This is my new partner,

Les Goddard. He's a summer hire and going to college to study bear biology. You might give him a few of your secret tips when we have time."

Turning to Les he said, "You're working with a great officer, young fella. I've seen her in action and she's all right." He turned to Betty, "Let me help you to the cabin with your stuff and then we can have some lunch and hot coffee. I've been grooming the horses. They needed it after the long winter in the wilds."

"We'll have lunch, Bill, but we should go up the ridge and take a look at where the bear is and what he's doing. I haven't seen him yet and I'm anxious to see this brute."

Bill took off his hat and wiped his brow, "You're going to be impressed with this one," he said confidently. "I wanted to shoot the bugger at first, but Ted asked me not to do that because he was so special. After I saw him, I had to agree. This old boy is the king of the mountain. Would you like me to ride up there with you and show you where to look?"

"Sure, Bill, but when we get there, we'll be doing our work and you should come back to the lodge. We'll probably be scouting the area most of the day and I know you have a lot of work to do." Betty was trying to let him know she didn't need his help but didn't want him to feel left out of the investigation.

"OK then, Betty. After lunch I'll saddle three horses. Do you need a pack animal on this trip up the mountain?" he asked.

"I don't think so, Bill. I think we can save that for later when we take more gear up the mountain. This'll just be a survey trip for us. I'd like for you to point out any other unusual stuff out there as we ride along. Can you do that for both me and Les?"

"Heh, heh, sure can, young lady." He busied himself with leading the way to his lodge for lunch, which he had on the stove—Ptarmigan stew. His specialty.

Bill was impressed with the way Les filled his third plate of stew and leaned back in his chair to cut off a chunk of chewing tobacco. "Did you like the stew, young fella?" he asked as Les pushed his plate back from the edge of the table.

"Boy, howdy," replied the farm boy. "Just like home on the farm."

"Well," continued Bill, "when you're ready we can go out and saddle some horses and ride up the ridge."

"I'm ready," said Les.

The men went out the front door and walked to the corral where three horses were tied to the rail. Bill pointed at the saddles in the tack shed next to the old log barn. "We can saddle up over there; easier to lead the horses than carry the saddles."

Les nodded and untied the three horses and

led them to the shed. He looked over the available gear and picked up a saddle blanket. "Which one is mine?" he asked.

"That one with the blaze on his face. Watch him though, he's a little frisky from his winter range."

While Bill began to saddle one horse Les worked on his mount. Once done he turned to Bill again, "Which one is Betty's saddle?" he asked.

"The one on the end. Higher back and more comfortable for her." Bill watched him saddle the last horse, impressed with the skill he displayed with the animals.

As they finished and leading the animals back to the corral fence, Betty walked from the house. "Thanks for saddling my mount, Les. I had to call Ted and report our progress." Then she added, "I think you should take a jacket with you. We may not need it, but the breeze off the glacier can get chilly around sundown."

Les nodded understanding and ran to the lodge to get his Trooper jacket. As he returned to the corral Bill mentioned to her about his skills around animals.

"He said he was raised on a farm in Iowa. I guess he wasn't exaggerating about that," she commented.

The trio mounted their animals and followed Bill out of the corral and up a well-worn trail leading to the upper reaches of the tall ridge above the lake. Bill knew the area well and led the way around the spot the bear had buried his kill. They stayed several hundred yards above the area where the dead horse was covered in an attempt to see the large bear. He was nowhere to be seen.

They waited, seated on the ground while the horses grazed nearby. It was early evening when they saw the bear come up from the brush in the canyon below.

Betty noted he was truly an animal to be admired and respected.

The trio sat quietly watching, as the bear ate most of the remaining carcass. When he'd finished eating, he stood and bellowed loudly, proclaiming this his territory.

Then, like a child, he walked back to where the horse was covered and lay down to sleep, knowing he wouldn't be disturbed before morning.

CHAPTER 4

It was early evening when the trio returned to the cabin, taking the saddles off the animals and feeding them some well-earned oats. After caring for the horses, they walked to the lodge building where Dover made coffee and asked if anyone was hungry. Ptarmigan stew was on the menu again. Both Betty and Les had a small bowl of stew and sat in the soft easy chairs in the large front room of the lodge. Betty busied herself with her daily report. Les sat quietly until Dover returned to the living room.

"I could tell you've been around horses in the past, young fella. You did a good job out there today. I guess I can trust you with my animals tomorrow when the two of you go back up the mountain," commented the old guide.

Betty had heard them talking and added, "We'll manage tomorrow, Bill. I plan to go up and scout the area a little before we watch for the bear to return to the food pile. There isn't much left of the horse, and I expect him to wander off to find another source of food. We'll have to follow him if he leaves the area."

"There are a few caribou further up the mountain, close to the glacier. He might want to try for one of them, but my bet would be for him to go down to the river to see if the salmon had arrived yet," opined the old man.

"We'll check out the caribou in the morning, Bill, but I think you're right, he'll probably head down to the river to check on the fish. This is an unusually large bear, and he may not follow the pattern. We'll just have to keep an eye on him." Betty Holden had followed bears in the past and knew just how unpredictable they are.

It was still daylight when the wildlife officers went to their rooms to get ready for bed. This early in the season, Officer Holden had not yet toughened up for the long days she was about to enjoy.

"What time in the morning, Boss?" asked Les as he stood to leave the room.

She thought for a moment, then said, "I guess around 0430. It'll be daylight and we'll be able to see to saddle the horses. Bill will have breakfast for us before we leave."

"I'll be ready. I can saddle the animals in the morning if you like. I'll come back to the lodge when I finish with them."

"Sounds good to me, Les. Good night," She responded.

It was five in the early morning when they climbed aboard their horses to ride up the ridge and attempt to locate the huge bear. The air was cool with only a slight breeze blowing down the slope of the ridge. As she expected, there was no sign of the big grizzly to be seen near the dead horse. The bones were scattered as if the old bear had searched the pile for one more meal.

Betty and Les rode up the ridge to the top and over to the tongue of glacier where they could see several caribou bedded down on the ice to keep cool. It was a peaceful scene and they climbed from their horses to sit and watch them for a while.

They had watched nearly a half hour when Betty suggested they move on and attempt to locate the bear. The officers climbed aboard their mounts again and rode down the long, barren slope to the trail the bear had been using to move up and down the slope.

"It looks like he's going to be easy to follow, but when he gets down the slope to the creek, that'll all change. I think he'll begin to hunt again and bumping into him while he's in cover could be a dangerous encounter. We need to be very careful. Don't let your horse panic if we see signs of the bear in the brush. I'm hoping he'll continue to the river and look for fish. They've begun to reach the river below the Russian River."

"You lead and I'll follow," replied Les. He followed her and her horse down the hill. They encountered several moose as they rode through the dense brush and on toward the Kenai River. They rode their mounts across a swift stream where they saw fresh bear tracks on the shore, but none were the tracks of the big brownie.

Following the edge of the mountains and moving upstream they finally were able to ride along the river flats and through the brush, to where the bears were likely to be seen fishing in the river. Betty moved her course closer to the riverbank, looking for any signs of the bear. Several miles upstream she came across a single track of their quarry in the mud near a gravel bar in the river.

"I don't like this at all, Les," she said quietly. "If he decides to fish here, he'll be seen by everyone in Alaska. When we start back, I'll call Sergeant Wilson and give him a report. We'll check this area and see if we can spot the bear, but we're going to have to start back to the lodge before long. It's a long ride back to the lake."

"I was thinking the same thing," replied the young partner.

As they searched the area for signs of the bear they found several fresh tracks near the river, but the bear seemed to be holding to the brush and trees for cover during the daylight hours.

An hour later the pair were riding back up the mountain toward the area they'd ridden through on the way down to the river. The brush was dense, but thinned as they rode up the steep hillside and angled back toward the lodge. Once on the hillside and in the open, Officer Betty Holden dismounted and reached for her radio. It was already set on the channel Sgt. Wilson had asked her to use.

"It's getting late in the day, and I was beginning to worry you had lost the bear. Where are you?"

"We're on our way back to Bill's lodge. But we did sort of lose the bear. He left the mountain and went upriver. I think you should have the Russian River officer go down stream to that flat area above Jim's Landing. We found his tracks there, but he seems to be staying out of sight, perhaps until nighttime."

"I guess we can't tie him up and make him stay on the mountain. I think you should get a good night's sleep and pack up in the morning. Call me when you start across the lake and I'll have someone come to get you. How's your new partner working out?" asked Wilson.

"Great, he's a smart kid and learns fast. He's going to be alright." She signed off and put the radio back in the zipper pocket of her jacket.

Back at the lodge Bill came out to take the gear off the animals and rub them down. He told the two wildlife officers to go to the lodge and get cleaned up for dinner. A half hour later he returned to the lodge building and walked directly to the kitchen where the two officers were sitting at the table drinking coffee.

"You guys had a long day. So did the horses. I gave them some grain and promised them a day off tomorrow." He laughed at his own joke.

"It really was a long day, Bill. The bear left the mountain and went upstream on the Kenai River. We found his tracks, but he was staying in the brush. He probably laid down for a nap before going fishing after dark tonight," Holden explained to the old guide.

Bill Dover thought a moment before commenting. "You know if he goes out into the river, he won't be a secret any longer. That big guy is going to get a lot of attention."

"Yes, I know. I've already called Ted Wilson to report that very thing. That means we'll be leaving the lodge in the morning. Can you give us a ride across the lake?" she asked.

"Gonna miss your company, young lady. I'm used to being alone, and enjoy it, but I liked having the two of you here for a while. I like that young fella with you. He's pretty savvy about my animals. Heck, I'd hire him to help me out right here at the lodge."

Les grinned with pride. "Sorry, Bill, but I already have a job." He snickered, "But if she fires me, I may come back and take you up on the offer."

Betty sipped her coffee again, "We'll pack our gear after dinner and be ready to leave after breakfast in the morning. If you need help with the boat or the animals in the morning, just ask. I really appreciate how wonderful you have been to us, Bill. I'll tell the boss to send you a tip when he sends a check for the rent."

"Ain't often I get good folks like you up here. It's been a good time for me. Come back any time." With that the old man went to the stove to dish up two plates of Ptarmigan stew.

The following morning Les went to the corral to help Bill feed the horses and get the boat ready for the trip back across the lake. Most of the gear was already on the dock to be loaded into the wide lake boat. The men finished and walked back to the lodge where Betty had finished packing the last of her gear and was sitting at the breakfast table. An hour later they had loaded the boat and were cruising across Skilak Lake toward the upper landing. As they travelled, Betty called Ted on the radio.

"We're on our way, Sergeant. We'll be at the landing in about an hour," she reported.

When they arrived at the landing there was a white state pickup on the ramp waiting for them. The uniformed officer standing near the truck waved to them as they approached. He greeted them as he helped unload the boat and transfer the load to his truck. They all said goodbye to Bill Dover and watched him head back to the lodge across the lake.

Once inside the state pickup Betty asked, "Have you heard any news about the bear?"

"No, but there was an officer in the area all night, just in case. She was checking fishing licenses in the area while she was there." The new officer asked, "Say, is that bear really as big as they say?"

Betty snorted with a stifled laugh, "And more," she answered.

He shook his head, "I've worked this area for several years and I've never seen a bear as big as they say this one is. I hope I get a chance to see it."

"Me too. He's magnificent, I've never seen one this large. I've heard there are bigger ones out on the Alaska Peninsula, but I've never worked out there. This one's big enough for me." She thought a moment, then added, "He's going to draw a lot of attention if he is seen by the public where we last saw his tracks."

There was little conversation on the rest of the ride to Fish and Wildlife Protection headquarters where they unloaded the truck into the garage area of the building before going to the office to see Sergeant Wilson and give him her report. Les followed her the entire time.

Ted motioned them into his office as they approached the door. "Did you have fun?" asked Ted as Les entered.

"I sure did," he answered. "Betty taught me a lot about bears. It was a good experience for me. Thanks for allowing me to go on this task." Ted only nodded and turned to Betty Holden. "I have some bad news for you, Betty. The bear came to the river early this morning and caused a tremendous uproar among the fishermen. His size didn't go unnoticed. By now he's on the internet and in danger of every poacher in the State of Alaska." He paused a few beats before continuing,

"Are you ready to go back up to the area and keep an eye on him?"

"Of course, Boss. Can I take Les with me again?"

"I had planned to do just that," he said. "Get some lunch and leave your gear in the garage. I'll have you relieved late this afternoon. Take your state truck and be sure you have slugs for your shotgun. I think there may be a big chance of bear-human contact when he goes out to catch his dinner. Stay on the radio, just in case."

"Will do, Boss. Come on Les, we've got work to do."

It took only minutes to load what they needed into her patrol vehicle. On the way back up the river she explained how they would go about watching the bear without being too public about it. If the bear was in the river, they'd watch from the trees on the riverbank. If he wasn't, they'd wait in the area of the parking lot and walk around the riverbank and check licenses. If the bear was seen in the area, they'd know soon enough.

She parked in a public campground area, unlocked her shotgun and slung it under her left arm. They crossed the road to the riverbank and began to check fishermen for bag limits and fishing licenses. They saw no sign of the bear but found a lot of fishermen.

It was late in the afternoon when there was a great deal of excitement on the riverbank just downstream from where they were working. Loud voices were calling, "Bear! Bear!"

Betty and Les walked downstream to where the fishermen were yelling excitedly. There, in the river, was a female brown bear with two cubs. The cubs were waiting on the gravel bar on the opposite side of the river while the sow waded into the water and stood up, waiting for a fish to swim past. It took only seconds for the bear to dive into the water with her huge head and retrieve a Sockeye Salmon which she carried to the gravel bar where her cubs waited. She dropped it on the ground and watched as the two cubs sniffed and then attacked the dying salmon.

Confident the cubs knew what to do she again waded into the river to repeat the process. Anglers, for the most part, watched from shore while the bear caught her fish, feeding the cubs and herself. Once they had their fill the sow led her offspring into the dense woods on the far shore and disappeared.

As the fishermen returned to the water to fish, Betty turned to Les. "I think we'll leave this to the night shift. It's time for us to get back to the office and make our reports. I'm about ready for some dinner, how about you?" she asked.

CHAPTER 5

There was no one in the office when they returned. Les and Betty went directly to their office to write the report. The report was long, and it took them nearly two hours to complete the document. Once finished, they drove to the local restaurant preferred by officers.

Froso's, the restaurant named for the lady owner, was noted for its good food and fair pricing. The coffee was good and the owner stopped by their table to welcome them. She spoke with a slight Greek accent but had mastered the language well.

"Officer Holden, good to see you again," she said in a pleasant tone.

"Hi, Froso. Good to see you, too. You know how it is in the summertime, we're always busy. It looks as if you're pretty busy yourself."

"Yes, like you we get crazy in here in the summertime." She looked at the front desk and said, "Oh, oh, I have to go back to work." With that she waved and returned to her desk to collect payment from a customer.

Betty took a couple bites of her Monte Christo sandwich and a sip of hot coffee. "Let's try to get out of here a little early in the morning. It takes nearly an hour to make the drive to where we have to go, and I'd like to be there if the bear decides it's time to go fishing. I'm sure the sergeant will have some orders for us, but he can reach us on the radio.”

The following morning, they met at the office at 0500, said sleepy hellos and climbed into the tall white pickup truck. They were nearly at the spot they’d park the truck when Ted Wilson contacted them on the radio.

“I don’t see any reports on the bear as of this morning. Go ahead and work the area as usual and keep your eyes open. Get back to me if there are any new developments.”

“Will do, Sarge,” she replied as they drove into the parking lot across the highway from the river.

“Let’s go to the river and work our way to the ferry crossing, cross the river and work our way down the other side. We might spot some sign of the bear as we walk back down river.” Betty was trying to be efficient with the hiking they’d be required to do on this journey.

“Sounds good to me,” replied Les. “We may spot him on the walk down the other side of the river.”

As they walked the riverbank and checked licenses there were many questions about brown bear sightings. Officer Holden answered as many questions as possible but continued to move upstream toward the ferry crossing. They were about halfway to the crossing when the Russian River officer called on her radio.

"Officer Holden, do you read me?" It was Officer Gayle Portman.

"Yes Gayle, I copy. What's up?" asked Betty.

"I just had a report of two hunters crossing the river downstream from here. They have a small boat with an Evinrude motor and crossed the river a mile downstream from me here at the landing. They told someone they were going after a big bear. Motorized boats aren't allowed on this stretch of the Kenai River."

"Oh, oh, it looks like the news is out. I'll try to get one of the drift guides to take us across to the other side from here. Keep me posted if you hear anything else."

"Sure thing, Betty. Out" Portman signed off.

Just above Holden and Goddard was a guide waiting for his clients to fish a short stretch of good water with fly rods. Betty called to the guide and he stepped ashore to speak with her.

"Hi, Betty, haven't seen much of you this year," he noted as they approached him.

"Yeah, Fred, I've been busy as the devil." She paused a moment and asked, "Do you have time to ferry me and Les across the river? I have a situation over there and I don't want to take the time to go to the ferry?"

The guide turned to look at his four clients, fishing in the river, "Sure, come on and get in. I won't be able to bring you back if you will be very long on your business."

"I understand. Thanks, but we will probably be quite a while over there."

"OK, come on then. Let's cross."

The trio climbed into the drift boat and the guide rowed them across the shallow stretch of water to drop them on the gravel beach on the other side.

"Good luck," he called as they climbed from the boat.

"Thanks for the ride. I'll make it right with you later. I appreciate it."

He waved and returned to the previous spot on the other side of the river to await his clients, who were still fishing in the same spot.

Once on shore Betty and Les began to make their way upstream through dense vegetation. Betty thought she knew the area where the hunters were located but proceeded with caution. Some poachers have no reluctance to take a shot at a game warden if they feel threatened. They saw several tracks of their bear as they walked the game trail through the woods.

Holden stepped out of the wooded area to the shoreline where she could see up the river. She had motioned for Les to stay back until she called him. Near the rocky shoreline she stopped to peer out of the trees to see upriver. She saw a boat beached a short distance ahead. Immediately she ducked back into the woods, held a finger to her lips to tell Les to be quiet and not talk. When she approached him, she whispered in his ear.

"I can see the boat pulled up on the shore upstream. They must be in the woods looking for signs of the bear. Follow me but be quiet. I don't want these men shooting at us."

Les nodded his understanding and followed her up the trail. They walked quietly through the trees and brush and could see an occasional footprint of the big bear in the worn animal trail as they made their way toward where the boat was beached. Just minutes later Betty held out her hand to stop her partner, pointing a finger to her ear to indicate she heard something. She took several cautious steps and stopped again, held out her hand, then pointed up the trail where she had heard someone whispering. She motioned for her partner to get down on his knees on the trail to keep a low profile while attempting to locate the voices. Then, she spotted the two figures ahead. They were both dressed in camo gear. Each had their rifle in hand. They were proceeding cautiously, listening for any sounds of the bear.

Betty motioned for Les to stay down as she stood and stepped into the open and out of the brush. The movement caught the attention of the hunters.

"How's it going, fellas?" she asked in a calm voice, startling the men.

"Where did you come from?" asked the lead hunter.

"I'd appreciate it if you men would put your safety on and shoulder your rifles," she said again in a calm voice.

The second man made a sudden move, but his partner held out his hand to stop him. "Sure thing, Ma'am," said the lead man.

Both men put their rifles on safe and shouldered them by the sling.

"What are you men hunting?" she asked.

"We heard there was a dangerous bear out here and we are here to take care of it. You know, for the safety of the fishermen," he explained.

"I think the two of you should return to the river where your boat is and put your rifles in the boat until we have a little chat about all this." There was an official tone to her voice, indicating this was not a request.

Les stood up, and the men were surprised to see not one, but two officers. The lead man turned to his partner and pointed back toward the boat. As they turned to walk back to the riverbank, Holden and Goddard followed them, a few short steps behind. At the riverbank the men complied and set their rifles in the boat.

As they turned to face the officers the lead man said, "How come you two are sneaking up on us and scaring us like that?"

"Before we go any further, I want to see your ID and your hunting licenses." Again, the voice indicated an order and not a request.

"OK, OK, but I want your ID too. A uniform doesn't make you an officer," said the indignant lead man.

Betty reached into her shirt pocket and opened the ID wallet she retrieved. She displayed it for the men to read, and demanded, "Now I've shown you mine, show me yours. Both of you."

She returned the ID wallet to her pocket and had her hand on the butt of the handgun on her hip as she handed the shotgun to Les. "Keep an eye on them, Partner."

Again, the lead man did the talking, "Alright," he said as he reached for his own wallet and motioned for his partner to do the same.

Officer Holden took the license from him and wrote the information in her notebook. She returned both licenses to him and took the same information from the second man. Both men had Anchorage addresses.

"OK boys, here's what we're gonna do. You two are getting in the boat, in the back seat. We're going to get into the boat in the front seat. You're taking us across the river, and we'll tie the boat up there. Then we're going to walk up the embankment and cross the highway to the parking area on the other side. I'm going to check your licenses on the radio and then we're going to decide what to do with you. Somehow, I don't think a two-man posse is authorized to hunt a bear in these woods. At this point I don't think I need to arrest you, so please refrain from rash actions. Got it?" she said, looking both men in their eyes.

"Yeah, we got it," said the lead man.

Several minutes later the quartet was back on the other side of the river and had walked to the parking area where Holden checked with dispatch on the status of the licenses of both men. Then she ordered the men to have a seat at one of the picnic tables nearby while she called Sergeant Wilson on the portable radio. She walked a short distance from the men to keep her conversation private.

When Wilson answered she explained the situation to him and told him her location.

"Have they given you any trouble?" he asked.

"They thought about it but changed their minds and complied. They admitted they were out to kill a 'nuisance' bear."

"What do you want to do with them?" he asked.

"They haven't actually done anything yet, but they admitted to hunting brown bears out of season and without a permit. I think we should take their rifles and cite them for hunting out of season and for having no permit. They can probably get their guns back after their court hearing," she said.

"OK Betty. Sounds good. I think you and Les should stay in the area for a while to be sure these men leave without any further incident.

Good job Officer Holden and tell Officer Goddard the same."

Returning to where the men were seated, she wrote each man a citation for hunting brown bears out of season and without a brown bear permit. The men said little during the process, but it was obvious they were upset and angry.

Minutes later she handed each man tickets with the charges listed. "I am taking your rifles. I'll give you each a receipt. You can ask the court to give them back. Do you have any questions for me at this point?"

"No. No questions," stated the lead man.

"I'll take one of you to your truck and you can go back for your boat. I see you live in Anchorage. Please drive safely going home."

Les sat in the back seat of the truck and the lead man sat up front with Betty. She drove him to his truck and let him out. Once the passenger was out of the front seat, Les moved up there.

"Well Les, what do you think of enforcing wildlife laws?" she asked.

"I have to admit it was unnerving facing armed men breaking the law with no backup and no way to call for help. I admired how you handled those two. It was a great learning experience for me. But I was scared to death the whole time."

"We all had to start somewhere, Les. We've all been in your shoes and had to learn the ropes.

You did good, young man. Now let's check with
Gayle and head back to the office to do the report."

CHAPTER 6

Betty and Les were at their desks writing reports of what occurred this afternoon, logging details of their encounter with the two bear hunters.

When she read the entire report on the hunters and their criminal history, she learned both had been arrested in the past for illegally taking bears.

Both had lost hunting privileges for three years, but had their licenses returned recently. It seems the hunters hadn't changed their ways and were attempting to find the large brown bear. This fact worried Betty Holden and increased her concerns for the well-being of the animals. She handed the report to Les and asked him to read it and give her his opinion.

"Wow!" he said as he finished reading. "It doesn't look like they learned their lesson and are back to their old tricks. Will the court use this when considering what to do about the tickets you wrote them?"

"I'm going to include this in my report when it goes to the court. I hope the DA notices that information and I'll make sure they speak with the DA when they file for a court date. These guys look like professional poachers to me," she said as she took the rap sheet back from Goddard.

"I've heard of people like this, but I've never had contact with them before. It's scary to think how dangerous the situation could have become out in the backwoods like that. It makes me want to be a lot more cautious when dealing with lawbreakers." Les had just had a lesson in law enforcement that he'd carry with him the rest of his life.

"Are you about done with your part of the report?" she asked.

"Yes, I am. I only need to make a hard copy for my own file."

"OK then, let's finish up and get some sleep. We'll be back at it in the morning."

Betty Holden was widowed when her husband was killed in a plane crash several years ago. He'd been flying a patient to Anchorage from Illiamna in bad weather when the engine failed and they crashed in Lake Clark pass, killing the pilot and his passenger. Since then, she'd made her job the focus of her life. She never talked about the accident, nor mentioned her husband.

"Let's meet at 0500 again, Les. I think we should go back to the same area to begin looking for signs of the bear. There are more fish in the river each day and he'll be looking for a place to get his share. We can see if Gayle has learned anything about new sightings."

"Sounds like a good plan to me, Betty. I want to thank you for being patient with me. I'm trying to learn the ropes, but there's a lot of learning to do and each day I see things I had never even thought about before. You've already taught me a lot and I'll try to learn more tomorrow."

Betty smiled, "Nobody knows the job when they take it, Les. Just stay alive until you learn the rest. I'll see you here in the morning."

Les was living in a rented apartment not far from the office. Betty owned a small house on the East side of Soldotna, about two miles from the office. Both officers were home within minutes and happy to be there. It had been an exhausting day.

Ted Wilson was in his office when Betty arrived at 0430. He called to have her come to his office. He asked for a short report on events the previous day. Betty recited the narrative of the report.

She sat in the chair opposite the boss's desk and spoke with ease with him. "I saw the report of their other arrest for poaching and this one looks to be nearly the same scenario. To me these men look like professional poachers who do this for money. I don't think they'll let this bear go. He's too big and pretty to let a 'hunting out of season' ticket stop them. Mounted, this bear would bring a fortune."

"I agree, Betty. But I want to caution you about how dangerous these men could be. They know you mean business and if you meet them out of public view the outcome could be disastrous. I want you to be very careful." Wilson had been in these confrontations in the past and knew how desperate some of these men can be.

"Don't worry, Boss, I've already warned Les about the danger. We'll work together to stay safe. He may not know much about bears, but he does know people and has a good head on his shoulders. He's a partner I can count on. But thanks for the warning."

There were sounds of movement in the other office. "It must be Les; he must be loading up. I'd better get back there and help him," she said as she stood to leave.

"Keep your radio close at hand," he said as he waved to her.

Les had nearly everything in the truck by the time she met him. "I brought a thermos of coffee for the drive to our patrol area. I hope you drink it black," she said as she picked up her shotgun.

The drive back to the river took almost an hour in the bright sunshine of the early morning. They had seen a cow moose with twin calves and another with a single calf as they drove to the parking area, sipping coffee from an insulated cup as they went.

In the parking lot they saw several fishermen preparing to go to work. The two officers slipped into the backpacks they were carrying, and Betty slung the shotgun sling over her left shoulder. She checked her zipper pocket to be sure the radio was in place. She nodded to Les, and they began the walk to the trail they would take upstream, checking licenses as they walked.

The first fishermen they met were airmen from JBER, Joint Base Elmendorf and Richardson, an Air Force Base near Anchorage. They checked licenses and asked if they had seen any bears this morning.

"No, but we've been hearing a lot of reports of a huge brown bear fishing this area at night," said the first fisherman as he put his license back into his wallet. "Is that true, about the big bear in this area?" he asked.

"Yes, it is," replied Betty. "I've seen him, and he is huge. I would guess him to be a record for the Kenai Peninsula. You fellas stay vigilant and don't approach this big guy."

"Don't worry, Officer. I don't wanna wrestle any brown bears." His partner laughed aloud at the remark.

"Just keep your eyes open and stay alert," advised Betty as she began to walk upstream once again.

It was early in the morning and there were only a few fishermen in the area. She planned to check fishermen as she walked toward the ferry crossing at the Russian River confluence. Les had said nothing during the encounters with the fishermen as they checked licenses and answered more questions about the bear reported to be in the area. It took nearly two hours to walk to the ferry crossing where Gayle was waiting for them in the parking lot with a thermos of hot black coffee.

"How was the walk up the river this morning?" she asked in greeting.

"Not bad, Gayle, but we had a lot of inquiries about the bear. I think he could be elected governor if he wanted to run."

All three of the officers laughed at that.

Betty sipped her coffee and then asked, "Have you heard any new reports this morning?"

"Only one. Two fishermen were coming back from the river when I parked, and they said the big bear was fishing in the river about a hundred yards from where they were fishing across from Lovers Leap. They said he watched them for a while before he stepped into the water. They reported the bear stayed for a little over an hour before going back into the trees. He's been gone almost two hours by now."

Betty turned to look at her partner, "I don't feel good about wandering around in the forest without knowing where the big fella's hiding. Let's go down the other side of the river and check the fishermen but stay close to the water. Later, on the way back we can go into the brush and look for tracks. That way we'll be close if he decides to go fishing again."

"Sounds like a good plan," commented Les. "I was wondering how scared I needed to be to say I didn't want to go looking for him."

Gayle and Betty snickered at his comment. The boy was learning.

They crossed the river on the ferry and travelled downstream for several miles. As they neared the spot where the fishermen had seen him that morning, there was a commotion on the riverbank. The officers moved quickly to see what was happening and found two bears in the river. One was the big brown bear, the other was a sow with two one-year old cubs in the river. The big bear was attempting to attack the cubs and the sow was determined to protect her offspring.

The sow was on her hind legs, roaring at the big male. One cub ran from the water and into the brush on shore. The other was in the water and seemed to be injured. The big bear turned to meet the sow, but she turned and followed the other cub into the woods.

The big brownie went into the shallow water to be sure the cub was dead. Satisfied the cub wasn't alive he allowed it to float downstream, then turned to follow the sow and other cub into the woods.

Betty pulled her shotgun from her shoulder and walked ahead of her partner. When they got to the spot where the bears had entered the woods, she followed tracks to see where they went and if they were still close to the river. Several minutes later she followed the tracks of the big bear who had followed the other two smaller bears, several hundred yards into the brush and trees. It looked to her like the big bear didn't want to follow the irate sow protecting her cub. He'd milled around in one spot for a few minutes then wandered off in another direction, probably to rest for a while.

"I don't think we should follow this bear to where he is going to lay down. I think we should just leave him alone for now. We need to tell Gayle to be on the alert and warn fishermen on the bank to watch out for him. He's going to be irritable today." Betty motioned for Les to follow her back to the riverbank. She took her radio from her pocket to call Ted Wilson.

"Officer Holden, what's up?" he asked.

"We just witnessed the big bear kill a cub in the river. The sow fought with him for a while to protect the cub but ran away when she saw him kill it. She and another cub ran off with the big one following them. He gave up the chase after only a few minutes. He went off into the woods, I presume to rest up." The report was brief but concise.

"Where are you now, Betty?"

"At the river. Les and I decided to go back to the ferry crossing and find Gayle to let her know the bear is in a bad mood. What do you think I should do now?" she asked.

"It's late enough now that after you see Gayle, just come on back to the office and do your report. I think you earned your pay today," said her boss.

"Roger that," she signed off and put the radio back in the zipper pocket.

"What now?" asked Les.

"You heard, we find Gayle, let her know what happened and then we go back to the office. We might even get finished today before bedtime. Come on, Partner. Let's hike back to the ferry crossing."

They located Gayle and gave her the message. She was kind enough to drive the pair back to their truck a few miles down the road at the Jim's Landing parking area. They thanked her for the ride and the morning coffee. She returned to her area to check more fishermen while Betty and Les drove back to the office.

CHAPTER 7

It was just after two in the morning when Betty Holden was awakened by the ringing of her telephone. "Hello," she answered in a groggy voice.

"Betty, it's Ted Wilson. I need you at the office as quickly as possible."

"What's the trouble, Ted?" she asked, her head now clear.

"There's been a bear attack at Russian River campground. Bring your shotgun and come to the office right away. I want you to go with me on this one. We have one camper injured and one dead. Gayle is on the scene. She called the troopers to investigate and an ambulance for the injured camper. She needs a hand with the gawkers. Have Les bring your truck to the campground. You and I will be flying up there in the trooper helicopter. I'll meet you at the office."

"Wow, Sarge! I'll be right there as soon as I call Les. I'll be there in fifteen minutes."

She called Les and asked him to go to the office and drive the truck to the Russian River campground. "Keep an eye out for moose crossing the road. You don't want to hit one with the state vehicle."

She dressed quickly, strapping on her sidearm and filling her jacket pocket with shotgun shells. She pulled her shotgun from the cabinet and started her private vehicle for the drive to the office. She found Ted Wilson sitting in his truck in front of the office. Shotgun in hand she climbed into his truck for the ride to the airport where the helicopter was waiting.

It took them only 20 minutes to fly to the campground, landing on the road near the camping area. A Trooper car was now on the scene, blocking traffic from entering the campground. The helicopter pilot didn't shut the engine off but motioned for them to exit the helicopter. Once they were away from the rotor blades the pilot added power and left the scene.

An Alaska State Trooper met them as they walked toward the campground. "Hello, Ted," he greeted as they approached. "I'll show you where the site is. Gayle is there waiting for you. She has a couple of witnesses to interview but wants you to try to find the bear. She's had a tough time keeping spectators away from the scene. I have two more troopers on the way. They should be here in about ten minutes."

"Sounds good, Ed. You go back to what you're doing and we'll find Gayle. Thanks."

When they arrived at the campsite, they could see the body of the victim on the ground, covered with a blanket. The injured man had been removed by EMT's. Gayle saw Betty and the Sargeant approaching and motioned for them to join her as she interviewed one of the witnesses.

"Hi Guys," she greeted as they walked to the scene. "Sarge, this is Mr. Morris. He saw the bear attacking the two campers. He said it was a sow with a small cub. When I got the call, I suspected it was the big brownie we've been watching the past few days. I have a statement from another witness who tells the same story as Mr. Morris. I think we should get these campers out of here as soon as I can get some help with   notifications. That sow may still be in the area. We don't need another attack tonight."

"You finish your interviews while Betty and I heard the campers out of here. Betty, you start here and I'll go to the other end of the campground. We'll meet in the middle and attempt to get everyone out of here in a short time. Keep your eyes open for the bear, just in case she tries to come back again."

In less than an hour the immediate area was vacated. Some of the patrons were angry about leaving, but by and large they understood the reasoning. Most were anxious to leave for fear of another attack by this angry bear. Only a few asked any questions about the attack, but the few who did ask wanted to know, "How come this bear attacked a sleeping camper?"

There was no immediate answer to that question and no time to waste by answering it. It was more urgent to evacuate the area for safety than explain the motives of a bear. Betty and Ted understood the camper's curiosity but continued to get them out of the area for their own safety.

The evacuees were directed to another campground a few miles south of this Russian River area.

The narrow river canyon prevented the sun from reaching the camping area, but a sunny day was dawning. The river seemed a strange place with no fishermen at the water's edge attempting to catch sockeye salmon that were so abundant. Betty walked around the entire camping area, her shotgun in hand, searching for the bear and her cub. She found tracks of an adult brown bear and cub near the river's edge. She couldn't determine if this was the one that had attacked the campers, but it was probable. She called Ted on her portable radio to tell him where she'd seen the fresh tracks.

"Wait there. I'll meet you there in a few minutes," he advised. "I have more Troopers here now. I'll have them search the camping area and keep people out of the scene. I know you know your business but be careful down there. The grass and brush are thick. You may not see her coming."

"You're right, Sarge. I'd really like another pair of eyes with me," her voice reflected anxiety.

Minutes later Ted Wilson arrived at the riverbank to join her in the search. It was light enough now to see the tracks plainly in the muddy riverbank.

"Looks like she and the cub crossed the stream here. I wish we had hip boots, but we'll

have to cross the river just like we are. Keep your
shotgun above your head," he said as he stepped
into the cold water.

Betty followed, doing as he directed,
keeping the shotgun high over her head, away
from the water in case she fell. They crossed the
stream without incident and found the tracks on the
other side where the bear and her cub crossed.
They found the well-worn trail on the other side.
She was easy to follow but they moved slowly,
knowing the brownie could have stepped off the
trail, waiting in the tall grass and brush at the
trail's edge.

They followed the tracks more than a mile
downstream to the confluence with the Kenai
River. The sow and her cub continued to move
downstream. Another mile downriver, she stepped
off the trail and disappeared into the bush. They
tried to see, but it was useless. It was impossible to
see any tracks in the brushy, spruce covered
surroundings. Ted and Betty looked for more than
an hour, with no luck.

Finally giving up the search, they walked
upstream to the ferry landing and motioned for the
operator sitting in the ferry with no passengers, to
come pick them up. When they crossed the Kenai
River to the parking area near the highway, they
called for one of the Troopers to come get them
and take them back to the campground. They were
both wet from crossing the Russian River and were
beginning to feel the cold.

Gayle waited in her car until they returned. They welcomed the warmth of the vehicle and thanked her for the comfort. She dug into her backpack to find another coffee cup and a full thermos of black coffee, which was still steaming. It tasted very good to both officers.

After drinking half her cup of coffee Betty asked, "Well Boss, what now?"

"Les should be arriving soon. We can go back downriver and try to find more tracks of the sow and cub. I want to remind you that the big bear is still in the area. I don't want to run across him if we can help it. Time is not our friend in this case. All these campers will be wanting to get back in the river to fish, but we can't allow it until we get these bears out of the area. The big brownie could possibly decide to go back downriver. The sow and her cub have been fishing in the area for quite some time and will probably remain here. I don't like the idea of killing them, but they attacked campers and would probably do it again." Ted Wilson took off his cap and scratched his head. "Do you have a better idea?" he asked.

"I wish I could think of one, but you're right. The safety of the folks on the riverbank is our concern. I do have one thought, though."

"What's that, Betty?" he asked.

"When Les gets here, he and I could try to find her in the woods downriver. She's had a busy night and could be resting out there with her cub. If we could find her, we might drive her away from the river with shotgun cracker shells. If she comes back again, we may have to shoot her and the cub."

Wilson scratched his head again "Do you think the two of you can find her and drive her off?"

"I don't know, but I think it's worth a try. And another thought. If we could get Fish and Game to put a collar on her and the cub, we could possibly keep track of them. Of course, that would entail finding and tranquilizing them and getting the collars on them. I don't know if they have the capability to do all that in the short time we have to work with."

"That's a good thought, Betty. Let me get on the radio and ask Fish and Game about doing just that. If the helicopter's still available, they could be here in less than an hour. Hold on. I'll call them right now."

Wilson took the radio from his belt and changed the channel. He walked a few yards away and talked with the head biologist in the Soldotna office. Betty couldn't hear what was said but could see Ted making his argument via radio. A minute later he returned to Betty, seated in the car.

"We got lucky. They have a couple bear biologists in the office, and they welcomed the chance to help save the lives of two brown bears. It will be up to you and Les to find them first."

"Les just called me. He's in the parking area at the campground. I asked him to come back

to the parking area at the ferry. I'll meet him
there. I'm almost dried out and I'm getting warm.
We can go back across the river on the ferry and
assume the search. He's a savvy kid and he's
learning quickly. I trust him to back me up and be
useful in the search. He doesn't know much about
brown bears, but he is woods- wise and has a lot of
nerve. I think we can find the bear, though I don't
have any idea how long it will take. Just have him
cross on the ferry and bring his pack and "tranq"
gun. If we locate the bears, we'll call him on the
radio. You can point him in the right direction
when he gets here. I'll be waiting for your call
when he does get here."

Just then, Les arrived in the ferry landing
parking area. The two officers crossed the river
once again. They followed tracks to where they
disappeared into the deep woods. Les said he
thought he could determine which way she went in
the brushy surroundings. Betty let him take the
lead in the search. They searched for more than an
hour when her radio squawked. It was Wilson.

"The biologist is here and I'm sending him
across the river. Good luck"

"We're downriver more than two miles and
in the deep timber near the foot of the mountain.
We're upstream from Jim's Landing in the woods.
Les said he picked up a trail that could be them.
Send him down here and have him call me when
he gets here. I'll direct him to where we're
looking."

"Roger that," said Wilson.

Les had just found the bears sleeping against a downed fire killed spruce log. He motioned for the two officers to move away, not wanting to awaken the bears with a human scent. They moved back nearly a hundred yards and waited for the biologist to arrive.

The biologist soon made his way to where they were waiting.

Whispering, he asked, "Where are they?"

Betty pointed in the direction of the sleeping bears.

Without another word he took off his pack and rifle. He loaded a tranquilizer dart into the gun and closed the bolt. He nodded at Les, who led the sneak to where the sow and cub were still sleeping. The biologist cupped another dart in his left hand and walked with the gun close to his shoulder. When they were close enough to see the bears, Les stepped out of the way and pointed to the sleeping pair.

The biologist stepped to the lead, put the gun to his shoulder and fired.

The first shot was perfect, striking the bear in the rump. Awakened, the sow bellowed, jumped to her feet and began biting at the dart. The biologist reloaded and aimed at the cub, who was awake and watching its mother bite the dart in her hip.

The second shot sounded. The cub jumped back a few feet and began to bite at the dart in his

rump. The sow pulled the dart from her hip and
began to run through the woods with the cub at her
heels. In less than two minutes she began to slow
her pace and stagger. At the same time, the cub
fell to the ground unconscious. The sow stopped
running and returned to her cub, sniffing it as it lay
on the ground in front of her.

It was clear she was about to feel the full
effects of the dart as she began to stagger. Betty,
Les and the biologist waited several minutes
before approaching the animals. The biologist
poked the sow with the barrel of his gun, but she
didn't move. Without a word he dropped to his
knees and took a bright orange color collar from
his pack. He fastened it securely to the large bear
and repeated the process with the cub. Then the
trio of officers stepped back into the woods to wait
for the tranquilizers to wear off.

Less than an hour later the two bears had
recovered. Bewildered by the drugs, they walked
slowly down the trail toward the foot of the
mountain, and further back in the trees.
When the bears were gone the officers high fived
the biologist.

"I guess I can introduce myself now," he
said. "My name is Gordon Ferril. It looks like we
were successful."

"I hope so," commented Betty Holden. "I'd
hate to have to come back here and destroy these
two." Turning to Les, she introduced him to the
newcomer.

“Pleased to meet you both. Your Sergeant has the tracking device and can keep track of them. If I'm done for now, I have to get back to the office. It was fun working with both of you.”

CHAPTER 8

Betty and Les walked back along the riverbank to the ferry crossing and crossed the river to the parking lot on the other side. Once she reached the truck, she called Sergeant Wilson on her radio.

"We finished the job, Sarge. What do you want us to do now?" she asked.

"It's late and you two have had a long day. Come on back to the office and write your report and call it a day. We have a couple of Troopers in the area and one stationed at the gate of the Russian River Campground. Gayle has gone home for the night, too. Did the bear give you any trouble?" he asked.

"No, that biologist was great. He helped us locate the sow and cub and then took the lead. He tranquilized both bears and put collars on them. He said you have the locators. Can you see where they are right now?"

"Yes, I can. She's gone downstream about a mile and is still off the river about a mile. I expect her to go back to fishing when she fully recovers from the tranquilizer. I wish we had a collar on the big male. We have no idea where he is now."

"You can bet he's not far from the river and will be back to fishing later tonight," said Betty. "My partner was a great help today, Boss. He should get an 'atta-boy' in his file for this one."

"Good idea, Holden. I have some work to do here in the office and I'll probably still be here when you get back. See you then,"

The exhausted officers drove back to the office and parked the truck. Betty told Les he was free to go home and get rested and she'd take care of the report.

"Are you sure you don't need me to help with that?" he asked.

"No, I'm good. The Sarge is still here. He can review it before I submit it to the office. Go home and get some rest."

"Same time tomorrow?" he asked.

"0500. We may find the bear at the river if we get there early enough." With that she went inside to her desk to begin her report.

Ted heard her enter the office and walked to her desk to speak with her. "Long day, eh girl?" he asked as he entered.

"I'll say it was, Sarge. I'm about done for today. As soon as this report is in the file, I'm going home to take a long shower and get some sleep. I told Les to meet me at 0500 and I don't want to be late." She stopped speaking for a moment to think, "That reminds me. Do you have any idea where you want me to start tomorrow?"

"I'll meet you here in the office in the morning and we can look at the locator to see where the bears are. If she hasn't come back to the river near the campground, I guess we can leave her alone for now. Just do your regular fisherman checks and ask if anyone has seen the big bear tonight."

He took off his cap and scratched his head, "You two did a great job today, Betty. I wish I had enough manpower to give you a day off, but unfortunately I don't. Try to find time for lunch and a little rest today. Get back to the office early if you can."

With that statement he turned to go back to his own little office down the hallway.

Officer Holden finished her report in less than an hour and put a copy on the boss' desk before going to her truck to go home for the night. She was totally exhausted.

Her body was still aching when the alarm awakened her the following morning. The hot shower and fresh coffee took care of that. She gathered her gear to drive back to the office. Les was waiting in the parking lot when she arrived.

"Ready to go to work?" she asked, laughing.

He held up his insulated coffee cup and nodded while climbing into the front seat of the truck. There was little conversation during the drive, but both officers finished the large, hot cups of coffee they brought with them. Gayle was waiting for them in the ferry crossing parking lot when they arrived.

"Want some hot coffee?" she asked, holding up a large thermos of steaming brew.

"You bet, Gayle. Fill us both up." She and Les held out their cups.

"Any word on the bears or the big brownie?" asked Betty as her cup was filled.

"I haven't had any reports yet this morning. I guess you're tracking the sow and cub. Has she come back to the river?"

"Ted's monitoring her movements, but as of when I left the office she was still over by the mountain with her cub. You know how they are. She may come back to the river with her cub during the day and fish that stretch near the highway where the tourists all take their pictures." Betty sipped her coffee.

"Well, I'm going back and open the campground for the campers. We have several 'Beware of Bears' signs to put up around the campground. Be safe," she said as she put the lid back on the thermos and walked to her truck.

"We'll be in the neighborhood if you need us, Gayle. Thanks for the coffee."

Betty turned to Les. "When you finish your coffee, we should cross on the ferry and start checking licenses as we walk downstream. I'm taking my shotgun and a pocket full of cracker shells just in case. With a little luck we may get another guide to ferry us across the river at Jim's Landing, saving us a long walk back to the ferry. Let's go young man."

Les just smiled and followed.

They asked about any possible bear sightings as they walked and checked licenses. They were writing their second ticket for fishing without a license when a young man approached them.

"Are you the fish cop?" he asked.

"If you mean Wildlife Trooper, the answer is yes. What do you need?" asked Betty.

"My dad is fishing downstream and sent me to the ferry to find you. There's a brown bear and a cub down there. They have orange radio collars on them. She's making everyone stay away from the river while she fishes for salmon and takes them to her cub. She's fun to watch, but dad's worried she may not like an audience and try to run us off. That's why he sent me to find you."

"OK, son. Les and I will follow you back to where your family is fishing. We might want to hurry along, though." She motioned for Les to follow.

A little more than a mile downstream they came upon the other fishermen huddled on the riverbank about a hundred and fifty yards upstream from where the bear was wading in the river. There were seven fishermen watching the spectacle.

Speaking in a soft voice, Betty spoke to the small crowd, "I think it would be a good idea if you folks would walk further upstream. You can see the bright orange collars on the bears and that means they're being tracked. The reason they're being tracked is because they're the bears involved in the bear attack at the campground the night before last. I'd rather not tempt her any further."

"That sounds like good advice to me," said the man with his arm around the boy who had summoned them.

The officers watched the bears from the spot abandoned by the fishermen, who had now moved another hundred yards upstream. An occasional drift boat full of fishermen drifted by but gave the bear a wide berth as they passed. The bear only stopped and watched as the boats moved steadily along.

On the far riverbank a large crowd of onlookers were watching and photographing as the bear fished and fed her cub. This spectacle continued for more than an hour until the bear carried a fish to shore and shared it with the cub before moving back into the dense foliage, away from the river.

Once the bear left the area, fishermen returned to continue their own fishing. This is a very good fishing spot for both bears and men. Les and Betty watched for another hour and were about to leave when once again, the fishermen fled the riverbank. They moved quickly upstream, away from the popular fishing hole.

From downstream came a huge brown bear. It was the giant bear Betty and Les had seen on the mountain. Les began to get on his feet, but Betty held out a hand to stop him.

"Let's just sit here and watch him for a while," she whispered.

Les nodded and pulled his pack from his back. He dug inside for his camera, a large digital Nikon with a huge telephoto lens. He rested the long lens on his knee to steady his camera. Snapping several still photos and one lengthy video, he put the camera back into his backpack.

I think I got some good shots of the bear," he said as he leaned close to whisper to Betty.

She nodded her understanding and continued to watch the huge bear. They watched him for more than an hour when he decided it was time to leave the fishing hole and return to the woods below this favored fishing spot.

Finally, she stood and turned to her partner, "Come on Les, let's go back to the ferry and head for home. I don't think the big boy will return today. I'll call Sergeant Wilson to let him know what happened."

Les was grinning broadly, "I'll print these photos and bring some copies to the office in the morning."

"Taking the pictures was a good idea, partner. I should have done that myself. After watching him this afternoon, I think he is closer to eleven feet than to ten. I've never seen any bear even close to that size on the Peninsula. He's a giant." It was apparent she admired the bear for its size.

Back in the parking lot, Holden contacted Gayle to let her know they were leaving and told her of the sighting of the big bear. Gayle thanked her for the information and said, "See Ya."

An hour later they were at the office where Betty wrote her report. Les had remained in the office without stating his purpose. She finished the report just as Les reappeared.

"I got permission to print the pictures on the office printer," he informed her. "Here are the stills."

She took the stack of photos he handed her. She looked through them and commented, "Dang, Les. these are good!"

"Thanks. I made two copies for you. One set for the report and the other for you to keep."

"The Sarge has gone for the day, but I'll see that he gets to see them." She was shaking her head, "This is one giant bear. I can't get over it."

They left the office together and parted ways in the parking lot of the office. She would need to fuel her truck tonight before heading home to a much-needed shower and dinner. It had been a long day and there would be another one tomorrow.

She was eating a sandwich in her living room, about to turn on the news, when her phone rang. It was Ted Wilson.

"I just read your report, Betty. The photos are terrific."

"You can thank Les for those. He has a huge camera with a very long lens. I think he even took some videos of the bear while he fished. We saw him catch a sockeye and carry it to the gravel bar and eat it, then go back for another. We watched him for more than an hour. He finally ate his fill and wandered off into the woods downstream from the direction of the sow and her cub."

"I know we're spending a lot of time on this bear. But considering the attack at the campground, we need to keep an eye on those bears. This has become a safety issue. Just stick with it for another few days, Betty. I know checking licenses isn't your favorite task, but it's useful. I see you wrote a few tickets today. Three for license violations and two for over limit on creel count. You were a busy team today. Congratulations."

"I'll be out again in the morning. I told Les to meet me at 0500, as usual. Thanks for the call, Sarge." She hung up and went to bed.

CHAPTER 9

The following morning Officer Holden met her partner at the office where he gathered his backpack and gear, loaded it into the truck and climbed into the front seat. "Mornin'," he uttered as he hooked up his seatbelt.

"Good morning to you, Les. You look like you're still asleep."

"Yeah, I was on the phone with my dad until very late last night. I called to tell him about that big brown bear and the conversation lasted too long. I didn't get much sleep," he said while yawning and stretching.

"I don't plan to do as much hiking today. We'll cross on the ferry and go down stream to where the bear has been feeding and watch for him. Did you bring your camera?"

"Sure did. It's in my backpack. I sent them by E-mail to my folks and that's what the conversation was about. My dad was thrilled with the pictures and my mom was worried about me getting eaten. You know how parents worry about little things like that," he said, chuckling.

She snickered at the statement. "Want some coffee?" she asked.

"Sure, I slept late and haven't had any yet."

She poured hot brew into his coffee cup, recapped the thermos and put the truck into gear for the drive back to the ferry crossing, an hour away.

They arrived at the crossing and carried their backpacks to the little craft. There were four other fishermen on the little boat when they climbed aboard.

"Good morning, Officers," greeted the operator. "Are you going bear hunting again this morning?"

Betty smiled at the man, "We have to keep the public safe," she said. "After all, we wouldn't want the ferry operator to get chewed up."

The other passengers laughed out loud. "That bear as big as they say he is?" asked the fisherman seated on the upstream side of the ferry.

"I don't know what you've heard, but he is a big one. I've been in this business for a long time, and this is the largest brown bear I've ever seen on the Kenai Peninsula, and I've seen a lot of bears," she said.

The man next to the one who asked the first question spoke up, "Well, I hope you keep that one away from us. I don't want to lose my fish to a hungry bear," again they laughed.

On the other side of the river the passengers climbed off the boat to walk upstream from the landing.

"Excuse me, fellas, but I'd like to check your licenses as long as we're not fishing yet."

The four reached for their licenses and freely showed them to the officers.

"Good luck with your fishing," she called after them as they walked away, each one carrying a fishing rod. One had a large landing net.

They waved as they walked away. She returned to the ferry to speak with the operator, "Have many fishermen crossed the river this morning?" she asked.

"No, not many. They seem to be shying away since the bear incident. But it's early and it will pick up later this morning. Are the two of you going downstream this morning?"

"Yes, …the plan is to keep folks away from the bear if he comes back this morning. We really are going to try to keep anyone else from being attacked. That thing at the campground was tragic. We'll try to keep that from happening again. I'd appreciate it if you'd send word down to us if any bears show up in this area." She said.

"I've been told to stop crossing if any bears are sighted. But if I get word of any, I'll send word to you. Orders or no orders, if there is a bear in this area it'll be my job to get them to the other side of the river, safely." The operator seemed genuinely concerned for the fishermen.

"Thanks, we'll see you this afternoon sometime." She and Les waved as they began to walk down the riverbank.

There were only a few fishermen on this side of the river. News of the bear had indeed affected the usual crowd of enthusiastic fishermen.

They walked down the river nearly two miles to where they had seen the bear the day before.

"What do you say we get back from the river and into the trees, kinda out of sight and just watch for a while?" she offered.

"Sounds good to me. I can take a nap while you watch." He grinned as he spoke.

An hour later they heard people on the other riverbank shouting about an approaching bear. Betty kicked the foot of the napping Les. "Wake up, Partner. It sounds like we have a bear coming to the river."

Les reached into his backpack for his camera. "Which bear is it; can you tell?"

"No, I haven't seen it yet. I see people pointing downstream and talking, but I can't see the animal just yet." She paused, waiting for the bear to come into view. Five minutes later it appeared. It was the mama and cub from the day before.

"I hope we don't have a repeat of the big guy coming back to kill the other cub," she remarked. She was using binoculars to scan the tree line for any movement. "The cub is staying on the shore and in the brush. The sow is in the water waiting for a Sockeye to swim past her."

The mother bear soon caught a fish and carried it to her cub, then returned to the fishing hole. As they watched, a brightly painted van parked on the highway above the river. It was a Channel 2 news team. They unloaded television cameras and other equipment at the edge of the highway overlooking the feeding bears on the other side of the river.

"Oh, man, I can't believe it. There's a television team over there taking pictures of this bear." Betty shook her head in disgust. "I guess the secret is no longer a secret, Les. I'd better call the boss and report it. He ain't gonna be happy,"

She put down her binoculars to fish the radio from her pocket. She gave her call numbers and spoke into the radio, "Sergeant Wilson, come in."

A moment later there was a reply, "Go ahead, Betty, what's the problem?"

"Les and I are downstream from the ferry watching the mother bear and her cub feeding at the gravel bar in front of us. A van just unloaded a television crew across the river, and they're taking video of her. I have no way to cross to the other side from down here. If you want someone to speak with them, you should call the Trooper from the campground. He's about five miles up the road, the last I knew."

"I guess we can't do much about that, but I will have the Trooper contact them." He paused a moment, then continued, "Have you seen any sign of the big male?"

"No, not yet. I hope he doesn't show up and kill the other cub. This has become far too public for everyone's good. I wouldn't like to see all that on the six o'clock news," she said, shaking her head.

"You and Les stay there and watch. If the other bear shows himself, I guess you can attempt to scare him away with a cracker shell. But it may not work if he's trying to get the female to mate. I'll call you back after I get the Trooper on the road. Out."

"Keep your eyes open, Les. I don't want that big bear sneaking up on us," she said as she dug two cracker shells from her pocket and placed them atop her backpack for a quick reload if needed.

Within fifteen minutes a Trooper car approached with its overhead emergency lights flashing. He parked near the camera crew and climbed out of his car. The camera operator turned to meet him and put a microphone in front of his face.

Neither Les nor Betty could hear the conversation taking place on the highway across the river, but the Trooper pushed the microphone away from him and spoke to the camera crew. The news crew appeared excited and were waving their arms and pointing to the bear. It seemed the camera crew was refusing to leave the roadway. The Trooper reached for a pair of handcuffs and the reporter immediately backed away. The cameraman did not. The Trooper used his radio, and the reporter and cameraman began to gather their equipment as they called someone with a cell phone. Minutes later the van reappeared, and the equipment was loaded inside. The crew climbed inside still shaking a fist and shouting at the Trooper. As the van moved away from the area Betty's radio came alive. It was Ted Wilson.

"What's happening, Holden?" he asked.

"It looks like the Trooper told them to move on. They didn't like it, but they complied. Didn't look happy about it." She paused. "Oh, here comes their van. The Trooper is still watching them as they're loading their equipment into it. The reporter is waving his arms and screaming at the Trooper, who's just standing there nodding his head. Now the van is leaving."

She chuckled, "We won't look good on the six o'clock news tonight, Boss."

"I'll talk to the Trooper Captain to let him know this was a safety issue, not a political one. This whole incident slowed traffic in the area and created a large crowd on the roadway. Between the danger from this traffic and the big male bears..." He trailed off for a moment then continued, "Just stay out of sight and in the area as best you can without being observed. And keep an eye out for that other bear. I don't want an officer hurt on this case."

"I understand, Sarge. I don't want to be hurt either. I guess we can stay in the area until late this afternoon. I think the sow and cub will leave the area when she gets her fill of fish. Yesterday the big bear didn't show up until after she left. I'm hoping he does the same today."

"Just keep your eyes open and be alert. He may just come from another direction and surprise you." Wilson had genuine concern for his officers.

Les and Betty stayed back in the bush and trees to observe the river and the feeding bears. She caught a final fish and gave it to her youngster, then she found a patch of grass on the riverbank and lay down to take a short nap. The cub fed on the fish for more than a half hour, then awakened his mother by biting her on the ear. She jumped to her feet and bellowed a loud growl. The cub jumped back to avoid a slap of her large paw, then ran up the riverbank and into the woods downstream from where the two officers were watching. The mother bear looked at where the cub had run for a couple of minutes, then followed her offspring into the trees.

"How was that for a sow, Les?" she asked. "Are you learning anything about how brown bears live?"

"I am beginning to think the bears are more social and more friendly than the people watching them. I did get a few more pictures, though." He held up his camera and flashed through the still pictures on the screen at the back of the camera for Betty to view.

"Nice photos, Les. I have a little coffee left in my thermos, do you want some?" she asked.

"I might as well, since we're just waiting for the other bear to show himself. Do you think he'll smell the coffee and come ask for a cup?" he quipped.

"No, I think he is going to be too interested in the fish in the river to think about us. I just hope he doesn't follow the sow and cub into the trees," she said in a thoughtful tone.

They were both quiet for a long while until Les whispered, "I think doing nothing is more work than being out here checking licenses and counting fish on a stringer."

She was about to give him an answer when the crowd across the river again became loud and excited. Betty turned her binoculars downstream just as the big male came out of the trees from the same direction as the night before. He ambled slowly toward the gravel beach he'd used before. He noticed the humans on the other shore and stopped several times to assess their possible threat. He stood on the gravel shore a long while before entering the water. He was up to his furry belly in the cold water, intently watching.

Suddenly he slammed his head into the water to come out again with a sockeye salmon in his jaws. He took the fish to shore and tore it apart with his teeth and claws, eating the fish eggs first, then feasting on the rest of the salmon. It was a gruesome process, but it was the way of the bears.

The two officers watched for more than a half hour as the big brownie repeated the scene many times, littering the small beach with half eaten carcasses.

He was about to enter the water again when someone honked a car horn on the highway across the river. It startled the bear. He stepped back from the water, walked in a small circle, watching the crowd on the far shore. Finally, clearly annoyed, he wandered back downstream in the direction he had come. He disappeared into the woods and the crowd on the other side of the river began to disperse.

The two officers waited for almost another hour for further developments, but none came. Finally, Betty looked at Les, "What say we get out of here for the night?"

"Come to think about it, I'm getting hungry. Is there a good place to eat around here?" he asked.

"There sure is, Les. On the other side of Cooper Landing there's a great place with really good food. The lady who runs the place is a friend of mine. How about we go up there for dinner?"

Les was entirely impressed with the quality of the food and ate the sandwich like the bear they had just watched had eaten the salmon. She paid the tab and they climbed back into the State truck for the drive back to the office. It had been a very long day.

CHAPTER 10

After a great meal and a visit with café owner Arden, the two officers made their way back to the office where Betty wrote her daily report. The report was a short one but described the actions of the sow and cub, as well as the big male. It included a narrative about the news crew setting up cameras on the roadway across the river. Once finished, she climbed into her truck to drive her weary self to her home.

She had already had dinner and only wanted to shower and go to bed. Tomorrow would probably be another day of watching the bear. The day would be unpredictable and long, just like today had been.

The alarm went off at 0400 hours and she hauled her tired self out of bed to make coffee. She'd just finished the coffee when the phone rang. It was Sergeant Wilson.

"Good morning, Betty. I hope I didn't wake you," he announced.

"No, Sarge, I've been up for a while. What's up?"

"I had a late-night call from Anchorage last night. It was someone whose friend is planning a hunting trip to kill that big brown bear. He and two friends are gearing up and plan to cross the river at Jim's Landing and hunt the bear. They're professional hunters and guides. They saw the pictures on the news and decided they needed to take that bear as a trophy. They plan to freeze the hide until fall and claim it as a legal bear. My informant was once a Brown Shirt Trooper and doesn't like the idea."

"Wow, Sarge, so you think the tip is genuine?" she asked.

"Yes, I'm sure it is. I want you and Les to hire a drifter to take you downstream. Get ashore above the Landing and watch for a private boat. It'll be a sixteen-foot aluminum boat with no motor, only oars. I don't know the registration number, but I have the license number of the truck they'll be driving. I want you to follow them and stay out of sight. If they spot the bear, I want you to do your best to stop this poaching. Stay alert and have Les stay by your side at all times. This will be a very dangerous situation and I don't want you to take any chances. I'll have the local Trooper keep an eye out for their truck. I'm sending another officer to back you up, but he won't be able to get there much before noon. Until then, stay vigilant and don't take any chances."

"OK, Sarge, I've been in this position before and I understand. These types have no concept of right or wrong. They seem to be dedicated to their own plan. I'll take care and I'll call if there's a need to contact the hunters." Betty was very worried about the task at hand. The last time she participated in a case of this kind, her partner was shot. The wound forced him to retire. It was a sad end to a good officer's career. "I'm leaving my house now to go to the office and pick up Les."

"Stay safe out there," Wilson cautioned as he signed off.

Les was standing beside his private vehicle when she arrived. She rolled down her driver side window to speak with him, "Did you bring me a cup of coffee?" she asked.

"Sure did," he replied, holding up a large thermos.

"Climb in, we have a big job to take care of today." He climbed into the truck and strapped on his seatbelt.

He poured her a cup of coffee to drink on the drive to the Russian River area. "What's the big job?" he asked.

She took the cup and sipped the coffee, "Good coffee, Les, did you brew this?"

"Yeah," he said, "Just plain old Hills Brothers Coffee. What's the big job for today?"

She explained her early morning call from the Sergeant and the plan to hire a drift guide to take them downstream to the spot where the bears had been feeding in the river. They would walk down toward Jim's Landing and wait until the hunters came across the river. "We won't make contact until they actively pursue the bear. This could be a dangerous assignment and I want you to stay close beside me at all times. I once lost a good partner in a case very much like this one. I don't want that to happen to you or myself.

There'll be three hunters in the party, and they could be dangerous. Also, we'll be in bear country. We need to be aware if a bear approaches."

"I'll try to be your right-hand man, but I'll be on your left side. Just give me orders and I'll try to follow them. I admit I'm pretty green, but I understand what we're up against." Les was beginning to get very nervous.

"I don't want to cause an incident, but our job today is to protect the bear." She paused a moment and looked at him, "You're a good man and should be a good officer if you choose to become one of us. You don't have any experience in this kind of situation, so just follow my lead and stay alert."

"You sound as if you know what will happen," he commented.

"A partner of mine was shot in a situation much like this one. I don't want it to happen again," she kept her eyes straight ahead and never looked at him.

They found her river guide friend at a private boat launch. It took only a few seconds to get him to agree to take them downstream and drop them at the spot she had described. The officers loaded their gear into the drift boat for the trip to the drop-off spot. Once ashore she thanked him and put the pack on her back but kept the shotgun in her left hand. She checked to be sure it was fully loaded and ready. Les followed her lead and checked his weapon. Satisfied they were properly equipped, she motioned for him to follow her down the trail where they would find a spot to await the hunters.

They found a good spot to wait, concealed by the vegetation. An hour later a pickup truck, towing a small trailer, backed down the boat launch to unload the small aluminum rowboat. Their gear was loaded into the boat and one of the men drove the truck to a parking area and walked back to the boat. He climbed into the boat and one of the other men began to row it across the steam. Though he rowed at a fast rate the boat drifted quite a distance before they reached the other shore. Once the boat was secured onshore the men unloaded their gear and began to slip into their backpacks. They checked to be sure their weapons were loaded and began the trek into the spruce forest to look for their prey.

Betty Holden held her finger to her lips to warn Les about being very quiet. It didn't take long for the hunters to get out of sight. She motioned for him to follow her. Slowly she walked on the same trail the hunters had taken. She pointed out a few broken twigs where the hunters had walked. The ground cover prevented them from finding any boot prints.

The hunters moved quietly and slowly away from the river. When they reached the spot where the mountain began to climb, the hunters turned downstream to follow the contour of the terrain.

The officers could not see the hunters but could hear them walking in the brushy forest. Holden held out her hand to stop Les, putting her finger to her lips.   She pointed to her ears and shook her head. Les replied with a nod.

The officers were attempting to learn the direction the hunters had taken. Suddenly, on the trail ahead, there was the sound of something in the brush. She took the shotgun from her shoulder, pointing it down the trail. The officers were kneeling on the trail now. Ahead the giant brown bear emerged from the foliage and was stopped, looking down the trail in the direction of the hunting party. He stood there for a long while, listening. After several minutes Betty and the bear heard the men walking on the trail again. The bear listened for only a moment and crossed the trail and disappeared into the woods moving in the opposite direction from the hunters.

Betty turned to motion for Les to sit on the trail and wait. She did the same and the two waited for nearly an hour before they heard the hunters returning. Les and Betty crept carefully into the brushy forest to hide. The officers were only about thirty feet from the hunters when they passed by. They didn't move until they could no longer hear them on the trail.

Finally, Betty whispered to Les, "Whew, that was close."

Les nodded but said nothing.

"I guess it's safe for us to follow the hunters now," she said, getting to her feet. "Same as before, we follow them. I hope they can't find the bear. But that means they'll probably be out here all day."

Hiking the well-worn bear trail was easy in this direction. The ground was still covered with leaves and vegetation, but the trail was deep and distinct, having been used for a millennium by bears, moose and fishermen. Like a freeway for game animals, it followed the river upstream for virtually the entire length of the river.

They were nearly two miles upstream, still following the hunters and getting very close to the Russian River Campground when they heard a shot ahead of them on the trail. They stopped and listened. Nothing for several seconds and then five more shots sounding as if they had come from more than one rifle.

"Come on Les, we have to find out what's going on now," with that she motioned for him to follow. They hurried up the trail and soon heard several voices ahead. She slowed the pace for the sake of caution but continued to move in the direction of the rifle shots. Soon she and Les could see the hunters on the trail ahead. Stopping to look with her binoculars she could see a small bear on the trail, and it appeared to be dead. One of the hunters was standing near the small bear. The other two were walking further up the trail about twenty yards to look at another carcass lying

in the trail. Betty saw it appeared to be the mother
of the cub and probably the same one causing the
mayhem in the campground a couple of nights
prior.

She motioned for Les to follow her to where
the first hunter was looking at the dead cub. She
had her shotgun pointed in his direction. "Don't
turn around. Just drop your rifle on the ground."

"What!" asked the startled hunter.

"You men up there, drop your rifles on the
ground, NOW!" she ordered.

"Not a chance, lady," said the leader of the
hunting party.

"That isn't a request. I'm an officer with
Fish and Wildlife, and I am ordering you to drop
your weapons right now."

The first hunter on the trail dropped his
weapon and turned around to see her. She looked
past him to the others.

"I said drop your weapons. Once they're on
the ground, we will talk about what happened.
Now! Drop your weapons," again in a demanding
tone.

The lead hunter looked at his friend and
nodded. They both dropped their weapons on the
grassy shoulder of the trail.

"Now move away from your weapons, and
you," she said nodding at the hunter in front of her.
"Move up there with your friends."

He complied, and moved to where his friends were standing. Les picked up all three rifles to lay them against a log near the dead cub.

"Which one of you wants to explain what happened here?" she asked.

The head man of the party spoke for the group, "I'm Burt Donnigan, these other two men are Lou Phelps and David Forsythe. We came down here to fish and heard there were bears in the area. We came out here to check it out before we started fishing. We were just walking up the trail when these two bears came out of the brush and attacked us. We had no choice but to shoot them," explained Donnigan.

"Keep an eye on them, Les. I'm going to be sure these bears are really dead."

Les kept his eyes on the three hunters while Betty checked the bears, poking a gun barrel in the eyeball of each one. She returned to the hunters.

"OK, fellas. I am going to seize your weapons and write you for hunting brown bears without a permit and out of season. You may get them back after your court date, but that is up to the court." She turned to Les. Get their IDs and write them up while I call the Sergeant."

Les lowered his shotgun and reached for his book of tickets. He took their driver's licenses and recorded the information in his notebook before beginning to write the citations.

Holden stepped a few yards down the trail to call Wilson on the radio. She spoke to him for only a few seconds to let him know what had happened, then returned to help Les with writing the tickets.

While she wrote she ordered the men to skin both bears, "Be careful with those hides, fellas. We don't want any holes in them while you skin them out."

It took nearly two hours to skin the bears and transport the hides to the hunters' boat. One hunter transported them, the hides and rifles to Jim's Landing where Gayle, who had been summoned by the Sergeant, was waiting to take them back to the ferry landing. The man rowing the boat returned to pick up his friends.

"I think we should get out of here before they get worked up and even more angry," said Betty as she loaded the equipment, rifles and evidence into the truck Gayle was driving. "Got any coffee, Gayle?" she asked.

Gayle was laughing aloud, "After a day like you two have had and all you want is a cup of coffee?"

CHAPTER 11

It was late when Les and Betty returned to the office. They still needed to draft a report, store the hides, and file the citations. Betty took care of the reports while Les cared for the storage of the hides. They would not be frozen until they were looked at by the Sarge. In an addendum to her report, she made recommendation notes to the court. Among them were revoking Burt Donnigan's guide license and hunting license, seizing the three weapons, jail time for all three hunters, and substantial fines. Usually, the court ignored recommendations of this sort, but in this case, they may agree because of the intent while illegally hunting the big brown bear.

The sergeant had gone home, so Holden called him there. "Hi Sarge," she greeted as he answered. "I've finished my report and we've put the hides in the cooler. I've locked the weapons in the evidence locker and tagged them. I cited them to Kenai Court on Tuesday to give the DA's office time to go over this report. Is there anything else for me to do tonight?"

There was a silent moment before he answered. "No, you two did an excellent job today. It could have been a very dangerous one and you two handled it well. Good job. I know you're scheduled to work this weekend and I wish I could give you some time off, but the truth is we still need to keep an eye on the big brownie. The men may not be the only ones looking for a trophy. Get some rest and make your start time a little later tomorrow."

"Sounds good to me and I know Les will welcome a chance to sleep in. Just call me if anything comes up." She paused, "Oh, and Sarge. Give Gayle an attaboy, will you? She was a big help out there today."

"I'll see what I can do. Good night, Betty."

Holden locked the office and checked her watch. Froso's restaurant was still open. She called out to Les, "Hey, Les, let's go to Froso's for a bowl of soup and a cup of coffee."

"That sounds good to me. I'll meet you there."

While sipping his coffee, Les told his partner that he had been scared the entire time they were in confrontation with the hunters.

"Don't ever get over that feeling, Les. It will help keep you alive. For what it's worth, I was frightened myself. But you can never let the perps know what you feel. A good bluff is worth more than a fast bullet in most cases. I want you to know you did a great job out there today, Partner. I hope you're learning about bears and people as well."

He was spooning beef barley soup into his mouth. He wiped his lips with a napkin before speaking again. "You know, I was hesitant about having a female for a partner, but I've learned just how experienced and knowledgeable you are. I've learned to trust you. I hope I can hold up my end every time we have to confront someone.”

"I have no doubt about you, Les. You’re a good officer and will make an even better one with more experience. Only time can do that for you,” she took another swallow of her coffee and called for the check. "See you tomorrow around eight.” She said as she took the bill to the front desk.

At home she went directly to the shower for a relaxing hot soak. The hot water spraying over her body made the tensions of the day disappear. She fell into her bed and immediately went to sleep.

The alarm sounded at six to awaken her to a beautiful sunny day. She drank a cup of coffee and put on a clean uniform. She filled her thermos and locked her house behind her. She drove to the post office to check her mail on the way to the office. The Sergeant’s truck was in the parking area when she arrived.

She was sitting at her desk when the Sarge walked in. "Good morning, Betty,” he greeted as he entered.

She looked up, "Good mornin’ Sarge,” she replied.

"What’s your plan for the day?” he asked.

"I guess we’ll go back to the fishing hole for the bears and wait. I’ve been thinking, and it came to me. That big brownie killed the first cub, probably to get the sow to mate with him. She ran off with the other cub, but he kept coming to the area. I think he was going to make another attempt to get the second cub and free the mamma bear to mate with him. I think it's possible he may leave the area when he realizes she is no longer there."

"That's a pretty good thought, Holden," he took off his cap and scratched his head. "Do you have any ideas about where he may go if he leaves the fishing hole?"

"Not a clue," she replied. "I've been thinking he may just find another female to follow around. There could be more females in the area around the fishing hole. I haven't seen any others, but they could be out there waiting for more fish to show up. I guess the only way to find out is to watch the big boy."

"Do what you think is best and keep me informed as to what is happening out there. I also want you to be extra careful. There may be other hunters out there looking for a trophy." He gave a short salute and left the office to return to his own duties.

Les met the Sergeant in the hallway. "Morning, Sergeant," he greeted in a friendly voice.

"Good morning, Les," he replied as he walked back to his office. "Good job yesterday."

"Thanks, Sarge," he said as he walked to Holden's office.

"What did the sergeant want?" asked Les as he stepped through the door.

"Oh, he just thanked us for a good job yesterday. We're going to be back out there today, by the way. I'll explain my personal theory while we drive back to the ferry landing."

An hour later they parked in the ferry parking lot where Gayle was waiting for them. "Hi guys," she called out to them. "I brought you some pastries. They had fresh apple fritters in the restaurant this morning." She held out the bag full of treats. "Have one on me," she added.

Betty and Les munched on the fritters as they loaded onto the ferry to cross the river. They began the long walk to the fishing hole, checking licenses of the few fishermen on the river's edge. She asked each fisherman if they had heard of any bears in the area this morning. None had, but some had heard about the incident the day before.

The officers were about halfway to the fishing hole when they came upon a family of fishermen. One child was standing in the water, close to what turned out to be the child's father. The wife and two other smaller children were sitting on a blanket on the high bank behind them.

The young fisherman was about ten years old and fished like a pro. While the officers were checking the license of the father the boy made a wild cast with his weight the proper distance up the line. The lad put so much effort into the cast he lost his footing and fell into the fast-flowing waters. When his head appeared above the water, the boy screamed for help. His chest waders were full of water and he was unable to regain his footing. At some point he dropped his rod and began to flail his arms about, attempting to swim without any success. He screamed for help and his head went under water again.

Les dropped his backpack on the ground and ran down the riverbank to a spot below the boy and ran into the swift water. He was able to wade out to where he could reach into the icy water, grasp the child and bring him to the surface. The boy sputtered and struggled to breathe. Les reached around the lad's chest and give a quick compression.

The action helped the boy clear his airway and begin a sputtering breathing process. Les carried the boy to shore and wiped his face dry with his sleeve. The boy began to breathe normally as the father and the mother reached the spot above where the youngster was now sitting on the rocky bank. Les pulled the boy to his feet and led him up the steep embankment to where his parents were franticly waiting.

The child's mother wrapped her arms around the boy and drew him close. She looked at Les with tears in her eyes and said, "Thank you, oh God, thank you." She was crying and hugging the boy close.

The father wrapped his arms around Les and thanked him with a tearful hug.

Les looked at the man and cheerfully said, "Sorry I couldn't save the fishing rod." They both laughed.

Betty was now by Les' side. I guess we'd better go back to the ferry and get you dried out. She took out her notebook and made some notes about the identities of the family and the heroism of her partner. They walked back to the ferry to return to their truck to have a cup of hot coffee while Les dried his clothes a little in the heat of the truck cab.

"That was quick thinking, Les," commented Betty as they sipped hot coffee.

"It was more instinct than thought, Partner," he said.

After an hour and a report to Sarge they again crossed the river and walked downstream. News of the rescue had spread among the fishermen and each one they passed thanked Les for his quick action. It was nearly noon by the time they reached the bear's fishing hole. They found a secluded spot from which to observe the happenings at the fishing hole. Les fell asleep for almost an hour while Holden kept watch. He was awakened by the loud voices of fishermen near the highway. They were pointing out a bear on the other side of the river, where Les and Betty were hidden.

Betty touched Les' shoulder and put her finger to her lips for silence. At that point a young brown bear, it was possibly a three-year-old bear, ambled onto the high bank overlooking the fishing hole.

It watched the people on the other side of the river for a long while before proceeding down to the river's edge and entering the water. He waded out to the first riffle and watched the water. He poked his head into the stream and came up without a fish. The second attempt came with the same result. He moved downstream a few feet and tried again. This time he came up with a fish, carried it to shore and ripped it apart with its sharp claws and teeth. He then returned to fishing again. This time he had more success and caught a fish on the first try. The result was the same. He ripped the eggs out and ate them first before eating the meat from the sockeye salmon. This continued for another three quarters of an hour before the bear returned to the wooded cover behind the river.

When the bear was gone Betty whispered, "Let's watch a while to see if the big boy shows himself. I couldn't tell if this young bear was a male or female. If my thinking is accurate and this is a female, the big male may follow her into the trees. It could be worth the wait."

Les nodded agreement and lay back down to rest once again.

Nearly an hour later the big guy appeared. He went directly to the riverbank where he sniffed at the mostly eaten fish on the bank. He watched the fishermen on the other side. Feeling no danger, he walked into the water to fish for a meal.

They watched as the big bear caught and ate several fish. Les had awakened and was taking pictures of the bear having his dinner.

The spectacle lasted another half hour, when the bear grew tired of eating and climbed the bank to the trail at the top. He was walking the trail when he caught the scent of something and stopped to sniff the air.

"I wonder if he smelled the other bear," whispered Holden.

The officers lay still in the brushy cover for a long while. It looked as if the big bear had lost the scent of the other bear and took a slow walk down river to the cover he'd used before.

Finally, Les and Betty gathered their backpacks and walked back toward the ferry crossing. They noted the family, whose boy had fallen into the river, had gone. The officers crossed the river on the ferry and sat in the truck for a few minutes to rest.

"I'm going to be happy to get home tonight," said Holden.

"I'm with you there," replied Les.

CHAPTER 12

There was very little conversation as they drove back to the office where Holden told her partner to go on home and get some rest. She would do the report before she left the office. Les agreed and went directly to his vehicle and left the parking lot as she went inside.

It took almost an hour and a half to complete the report including the sighting of the big brown bear and an account of Les saving the boy in the river. By the time she finished she was very tired and ready to go home for a good night's sleep.

The following morning, she awakened and made bacon and eggs for breakfast before getting into her uniform. She had always worked long hours in the summertime and the salmon were running, but this year the challenge of watching the giant brown bear had become a grueling assignment. She filled her thermos bottle and drove to the office.

Sergeant Ted Wilson was in his office when she arrived at 0430. He called out to her as she entered, "Betty, come in here a minute."

She stopped at his door and waved to him as he sat at his desk. "What's up Boss?" she asked.

"I just wanted to tell you that I read your report from yesterday and I am going to ask the Colonel for a commendation for your partner. That was a miraculous rescue he made yesterday.

He was lucky he didn't succumb to the cold water in the process."

"We had to go back to the truck and warm up after the incident. It got us downriver a little later than we had planned, but it worked out. There was another young bear in the area that fished a while before going off into the trees. Not long after it left the big guy showed up and fished for over half an hour. He then took a short snooze, and walked downriver like he has done in the past. Les got some great pictures. I don't know for sure, but it could be the young bear that came to the fishing hole is a female. The big brownie stopped and sniffed the air when he started down the trail. I thought at the time he may have gotten a whiff of a female and it was where the young bear crossed into the trees. I couldn't determine the sex of the young bear, but it could be a female."

"It sounds like a good observation, Holden," he said, scratching his head. "I know you two have been putting in a lot of hours, but we're short-handed, as always this time of year. I think this big bear is worth the effort to keep an eye on it. You citing those hunters is proof that it was certainly needed. Unless there's a change in the bear's habits, I want you to continue with this surveillance through the weekend."

"I don't have any other plans, Sarge. I don't know about Les, but I think he likes the duty."
She smiled, "I think he'll like the overtime, too."

"Is there anything you need?" he asked.

"No, I packed some MRE's for lunch today. I'll probably make us some sandwiches and perhaps a cake for the weekend. I was too tired to do it last night."

"How are you and Les getting along?" asked the Sergeant.

"He's young and hasn't had much training, but he's a quick study and catches on pretty fast. I've learned that he's a partner I can trust to cover my back. His actions yesterday tell you he's a quick thinker and a doer. I don't know what he plans for the future, but the department should hire him as soon as he finishes college." She had not exaggerated on his behalf. She liked Les and admired his courage, both in the rescue and with how he performed as backup in the poaching incident.

"I agree with your assessment, Betty. Now, hit the road and have a good day. Try to keep your partner out of the river." He said with a grin.

Half an hour later the two officers were at the ferry crossing sipping coffee while waiting for the ferry. Gayle drove into the parking area, stepped out of her truck and greeted them with a wave and a smile. "Mornin'," she greeted as she walked toward them.

"Good morning, Gayle," they replied. "Anything happening this morning?" asked Betty.

"There seems to be a lot more fish coming in and a whole lot more fishermen. I think it's going to be a very busy day."

"We'll be going downstream again today. We're supposed to keep an eye on the big bear." Holden stopped a moment to sip her coffee, "Have you heard any more from the three hunters?" she asked.

"No, I haven't, but if I were you, I would sure keep my eyes open. They didn't look like the kind to give up."

"I think you're right there, Gayle. It looks like the ferry's loading. If I need you, I'll call on the radio. See ya later." With that the two officers boarded the ferry to cross the river and go to work.

Following the bear trail downstream they checked licenses and spoke with fishermen. Most of them were good natured about being stopped and asked for their license, but one elderly man was grouchy about being interrupted in his fishing. He showed his license and immediately went back into the river to continue fishing.

They were only about a half mile from the bear's fishing hole when Betty held out her hand to stop Les. She pointed down the trail ahead of them. There, about a hundred yards away was the young bear that looked like the one they had seen yesterday. From this angle they could tell this was a female bear. Both officers kneeled on the trail in order to be less visible in case the bear turned around. She continued down the trail to the fishing hole.

The two Fish and Wildlife Officers followed cautiously, stepping off the trail and into the brush to hide as they neared the fishing hole. Holden took her binoculars from her pack and watched the bear walk down the steep bank to the gravel shoreline below. There was a small crowd of people on the other shore, and she watched them for a few minutes before stepping into the river. She was intent on fishing and catching a few sockeyes when another bear appeared on the high riverbank. It was the big male brownie. He stopped on the edge of the high embankment and spotted the female. He watched the other bear for a few minutes and made a grunting sound as he made his way to the water.

The female heard the bear coming and turned to meet him. The big bear heard the gruff warning she had issued and turned to walk a few yards downstream. He waded into the water and began to fish. She watched him for a few more minutes and then returned to fishing in her spot. She caught a fish and waded to shore for her feast. This was repeated over and over again for more than an hour. Finally, she had eaten her fill and climbed the bank to the trail at the top.

She looked down at him in the water one more time and crossed the trail to enter the woods leading to the mountainside. As she walked into the wooded cover, the big bear turned to climb the bank and followed her into the dense trees.

Once they were both gone from sight, Betty turned to her partner, "How about that, Les?" She was grinning broadly, "Can you get a date that easily?"

He chuckled, "Nope, not me." Now they were both laughing quietly.

They spent the afternoon taking turns napping and sipping coffee from her thermos. The MRE lunch menu wasn't exciting, but it wasn't bad. It did cure the hunger that had mounted while waiting and watching for the bears to return.

Late in the afternoon the bears returned to the river and were fishing together. They fished for about a half hour before moving back into the woods.

"Well, what do you think, Partner?" asked Holden. "I think the lovers are done for today, don't you?"

"That sounds likely. What now?" he asked.

"Let's check some more licenses and count creels on the way back to the ferry crossing. When we get there, I'm going to call Gayle and let her know we're leaving for the day." Betty stood and stretched her aching back. "Let's head back, Partner."

When they finally reached their truck and put their gear in the back seat, Betty called the office on the radio to report they were leaving the area. The sun was still high in the sky as they began the drive back to the office. Betty Holden was deep in thought while driving and following another pickup truck when her attention was drawn to a yearling moose feeding on the side of the road.

She slowed and pulled back from the truck she had been following when the moose suddenly ran onto the roadway in front of the truck she had been following.

She hit the brake pedal hard and swerved to the left to avoid striking the truck in front of her which struck the moose which, in turn, fell onto the hood of the truck and bounced into the windshield. The windshield shattered covering the driver and his passenger with broken glass.

Betty immediately turned on her blue overhead lights, passing the slowing truck. She pulled to the side of the road and jumped out of her truck, "Grab some flares and take them up the road to warn the traffic," she ordered while running to the damaged vehicle. The moose was still lying on the hood and appeared to be dead. She opened the driver side door to see two men inside. The passenger seemed to be unconscious and covered with blood. The driver was groggy and attempted to wipe the broken glass from his face, which was severely cut in the accident.

"Hold on, don't wipe your face. I'll get something to wipe the glass off your face. Just sit still a minute while I check your partner," she ordered.

She walked to the other side of the truck and forced the door open. She could see the man was breathing and had a bad bruise on his face where a hoof of the moose had come through the windshield and struck him.

She saw Les returning and called to him, "Les, get the medical kit from our truck." She thought it best not to detach his seatbelt for the time being. She checked the pulse of the injured passenger and found it to be fast, but regular.

As she returned to check on the driver, she saw a hand towel on the back seat. She used it to wipe the glass and blood from the driver's face. "Just hold on a few minutes, Sir. You have some bad cuts, and I'm going to try to clean the glass out of them." She began to wipe his face and put pressure on the worst of the cuts to slow the bleeding.

Les was tending the passenger now, wiping glass from the face of the unconscious man. He opened the medical kit and took a handful of gauze pads to clean the man's face. He looked at Betty and reached into the medical kit for another handful of pads to hand over to her.

Betty took the pads, wiped the man's face as best she could, placed several pads into a thick pile and told the driver to hold it in place.

She took her radio out of her pocket and called dispatch for an ambulance and a Trooper. "The passenger is out cold, and the driver has severe cuts to his face," she reported.

The passenger was beginning to moan and regain senses. She returned to the driver and took several more cloth pads to replace the blood-soaked ones on his face.

The accident scene was beginning to back traffic up behind it. Holden stepped away from the wrecked truck and began to direct traffic. The scene was chaotic for several minutes with the wrecked truck blocking one lane of the highway. Finally, she heard a siren approaching and knew help was about to arrive.

The passenger was trying to move, but in his groggy state, couldn't understand he was still strapped into his seatbelt. "Don't let him unhook the seatbelt, Les," she ordered.

When the trooper arrived at the scene, Holden asked him to help in getting the traffic moving. It was backed up for almost a mile to the north and at least a half mile to the south. He held up a hand to stop the cars to the south of the wreck while, at the same time, motioning for the southbound traffic to keep moving. By the time the strings of cars were moving, the ambulance arrived and medics began to treat the two patients. Five minutes later they were loaded in the ambulance and headed back toward town and the hospital. The Trooper summoned a wrecker to tow the car while Betty called her office to get someone on the list to come for the moose carcass.

It took another hour of directing traffic before the wrecker loaded the broken vehicle and drove away. It had been a long afternoon in a day that was supposed to end early.

At the office she sat at her desk to compose her report. It took almost an hour to finish and make a copy for the sergeant to read. She was happy to finish and drive home for a relaxing evening.

CHAPTER 13

It was late Saturday evening in a large home in the center of the Muldoon district of Anchorage, an area of large, private homes. This particular home was on a very large lot with storage sheds for equipment and machinery. This shed contained boats, four-wheel transportation, canoes, small trailers and hunting gear such as tents, sleeping bags and packing equipment. This was the home of hunting guide Burt Donnigan.

In the lower level of the house Donnigan and his two friends, Lou Phelps and David Forsythe, were drinking a beer and planning another trip. They had a court date set for Tuesday in Kenai court.

"I don't care what that lady Trooper said, I'm going to get that big bear. I've hunted all over this state and this one is one of the largest I've ever seen. It's definitely the largest I've ever seen on the Kenai Peninsula. In addition, he's a beautiful bear. I want him and I'm going to get him."

"I know you want him, Burt. But how are we going to get there without drawing attention to what we're doing?" asked Lou.

"I've given this a lot of thought and I think we can take some large backpacks with tents and sleeping bags to conceal our weapons. We've seen the area and we won't need rifle scopes, just iron sights will do what we need. We will probably be close, and I think my light-weight sheep rifle will be just right. It's a .338 and because of the light weight, kicks like a mule, but has penetration power and will do the job on that bear if we place the shot in the heart and stay away from the shoulder bones." Donnigan outlined his plan, gesturing as he spoke to indicate the bullet placement.

Forsythe was nodding as the guide spoke. "You know, Burt? That might just work. But what if we do get the bear? How do we get the hide back here?" he asked.

"I've thought about that, too. We put it in the boat and float downstream past Jim's Landing, to the trail that goes up to the Kenai Canyon trailhead. One of us can pack the hide up to the parking area while the other two of us try to float down the rapids in the canyon to the lake where the one who packed the hide can pick us up. I have an electric motor to get us across the lake from where we enter the lake from the river to the upper landing. The motor is small, and will take quite a while to get there, but the one picking us up will need a lot of time to climb the trail and drive to the landing." It was plain to see Burt had given this a lot of thought.

Lou took a drink of his beer, "I'm going to volunteer to drive the truck and carry the hide up the trail. I don't want to be the one attempting to take the aluminum boat down the rapids and through the canyon. It could be very risky," he said.

Forsythe laughed, "Where's your sense of adventure, man?" he said as he took a swig of his own beer.

All three men laughed. The conversation went on for another hour while the plan was refined, and a plan made. It would take place on Wednesday, the day after they would appear in court. A plan was in place and the men went to the shed to begin gathering the equipment they'd need to make the hunt. They loaded the equipment, gathered food and water supplies to be placed inside a large, refrigerated cooler, until the day of the hunt.

The beer drinking and laughing went on for several more hours. Too inebriated to drive, Burt let them stay in his spare room, which he normally reserved for clients.

Burt had breakfast ready when the two guests came into the kitchen. He'd made pancakes, link sausage and eggs. None of the men seemed to be hung over and were still in good spirits.

Ted Wilson had given his two officers Sunday off, knowing how many long hours they had put in during the week. Gayle would get a day off on Monday but would have to be in the area on Tuesday to cover for the officers, who would be in court for the hearing for the hunters. Betty and Les would be responsible for covering her patrol area on Monday.

Monday morning Holden and Les Goddard began their day at the Russian River Campground. They walked the trail alongside the river to the falls and back again, checking licenses and counting fish on stringers. Once back at the parking area they drove to the ferry crossing and did the same duty along the Kenai River to the area where the bears liked to fish. They asked if anyone had seen any bears this day, but no one had.

It was nearly noon when she had a radio message from the Sarge. "Holden, can you meet me at the airstrip in about a half hour?"

Betty checked her watch. "I think I can make it by then, what's up?"

"Nothing special, but I thought I would buy you and Les lunch at Sunrise Inn, if you can make it."

"We'll go anywhere for food, Sarge. Do you want us to pick you up at the airstrip?" she asked.

"Sure, that would be great," he said.

She turned to Les, "Looks like we get a free lunch today, Partner." They both laughed.

It took about twenty minutes for them to walk back to the ferry. Luckily it was on their side of the river and crossed as soon as they arrived. They were only a few minutes late to pick up the Boss.

At the airplane, they exchanged pleasantries and loaded into the Fish and Wildlife truck for the short drive to the restaurant run by that pleasant lady named Arden. She'd worked hard to build this into a quality place to eat, whether it would be a snack, sandwich or a steak dinner with drinks.

While they waited for the waitress to take their order, the sergeant asked, "Well, how's your day going? Have you seen any bears yet?"

"No, but we will probably see them this afternoon. The big bear made an appearance yesterday in the late afternoon. I'm hoping we'll get to see him later today."

"You remember, of course, that you have court tomorrow?" mentioned the sergeant. "These guys are bad news, and I'd hate to see them get off because we weren't there to answer the judge's questions."

"We'll be there, Sarge. Have you talked with the DA about the case?"

"He called me to ask a few questions about it. He said it would be a pretty straightforward case and shouldn't be a problem. He asked me about the weapons, and I recommended we take them and get as large a fine as possible. These men are professional poachers, not just hunters that made a mistake or fishermen who were surprised by bears. This was a deliberate act of poaching." He shrugged his shoulders. "Who knows what the judge will say."

Their lunches arrived and they stopped shop talk for now. After lunch they drove Sergeant

Wilson back to his airplane and watched him take off. He wagged his wings as he departed.

"Well, Partner, that was a nice break, but now it's time to get back to work."

They returned to the ferry crossing. It was midafternoon and a fresh batch of fishermen were on the riverbanks. They checked licenses and counted fish for another hour before heading back to their hideaway spot near the bear's fishing hole. Half an hour later the big bear appeared and walked directly into the water. He caught a salmon and carried it to a dry spot where he ripped it open to eat the eggs before devouring the rest of the fish. He was waiting for his second fish to get close when the young female bear appeared on the high bank above him. She watched him a few moments before starting down the embankment. She walked to a spot several yards below him and waded into the water. The big bear only ignored her. He ate two more fish and climbed the bank to cross the trail and disappear into the woods on the other side.

A half hour later the female climbed the high bank and followed the same path into the trees.

"Ain't love grand?" quipped Les.

Betty laughed aloud, "I didn't know you were old enough to remember that quote," she said. "Come on, let's get out of here for the night. We have a long day tomorrow with court in the afternoon. We can meet with the sergeant in the morning and catch up on some paperwork before court. No need to show up before 0800 tomorrow. You deserve a later day."

The following morning, she came to the office at 0700 and drafted a report before meeting with the Boss Man. "Have you heard anything from the DA or the court this morning, Sarge?" she asked.

"No, but I'll let you know if they call. I see you have some tickets to file this morning. You might as well get on with that until after noon. Court is set for one o'clock. Don't be late," he cautioned.

Holden and her partner were in the lobby of the court when the session was called. They sat in the gallery while the official proceedings began. The case of the three poachers was the first on the docket today. When all the dignitaries were seated, the judge read the charges.

The judge looked at the defense table, "How do you plead to these charges?" he asked.

"My clients plead guilty, Your Honor. They ask for leniency in this case because they thought they were doing a public service in ridding the fishing area of dangerous bears. I have explained that this will never be tolerated." The lawyer had made his case.

The judge made some notes in the file before raising his head to look again at the defendants. "It is difficult for me to believe that these men didn't know it was wrong to shoot the bears, especially so close to where the public was fishing in the river. I fine each man $1,000. I revoke their hunting privileges for three years and forfeit their firearms to the State of Alaska. Arrange for payment with the clerk of the court. Next case."

The three men and their lawyer stood. "Are you satisfied with the judgement?" asked the lawyer.

"Yessir," said Donnigan, "Go ahead and pay the fines. We'll pay you for them along with your fees after court."

"They will want your hunting licenses, too," the lawyer advised.

Each man pulled out his hunting license and gave them to the attorney. He then went to the court clerk, paid the fines, and gave her the licenses. When finished he returned to the defense table to gather his papers and usher the men out of the courtroom.

Before the next case was introduced the two Fish and Wildlife Protection officers exited the courtroom.

"They didn't put up much of a fuss," said Les.

"No, they didn't. I'm surprised, but it makes me suspicious that they may not be finished with their shenanigans," said Betty in a quiet voice.

In the truck he asked, "It sounds like you don't think these men are going to quit illegal hunting."

"No, I don't think they are done with poaching. I'd be surprised if they didn't already have a plan to go after the big bear. I could be wrong, but I don't think this was much of a deterrent for them. These guys are professional hunters, and they won't let something like lack of a license stop them from going after that trophy," Holden had a worried look on her face. "Let's go to the office and report to the Sergeant."

In the office she went directly to Wilson's office to report on the court proceedings. He listened carefully to her, then asked, "What's your take on this, Holden?"

"To tell you the truth, Sarge, I think they already have a plan to go after the big bear. These guys never even flinched at paying the fine or at losing their hunting privileges, to say nothing of losing some valuable rifles. No, I think they already have a plan to get the bear," she was shaking her head in disgust.

Ted Wilson took off his cap and scratched his head, put his cap back on and looked at his officers. "I hate to say I agree with you, but I think you're right. Take the rest of the day off and get some rest. You can get back on the job tomorrow. I think I'll call the Colonel and discuss this with him. I'll let you know what he says."

It was midafternoon. Holden and Goddard had household chores to catch up on.

"See you in the morning, Les," she said.

"See you in the morning," he replied.

CHAPTER 14

It was just 0500 when FWP Officer Betty Holden entered the office to gather some papers and sign in for the day. She had taken a topographical map from the drawer and opened it on her desktop when Les Goddard entered.

"What's the plan for today?" he asked.

"I'm not sure, but I guess we check licenses and count catches like we normally do," she replied.

"What's the map for?" asked Les.

"Oh, I was just trying to figure out what they would do if they decided to come back for the bear. I figure, with backpacks and firearms, they won't use the ferry but will bring a boat of some kind. I think they may use an inflatable or even the little aluminum rowboat they used before. It just puzzles me as to how they'll get across the river, shoot our bear and skin it out, then take the hide that weighs more than a hundred pounds, and get back to their vehicle without anyone noticing. I can't figure it out." She stared at the map, perplexed.

"Why wouldn't they just load the hide and themselves into the boat and go downstream to unload it somewhere else?" he asked.

"That's what has me puzzled," commented Holden. "It would be an extremely dangerous risk for them to go downstream, through the white water in the canyon in their boat, unless they did use an inflatable. Even then, it would be a dangerous trip." She paused and folded the map, placing it back in the drawer. "Oh well, I guess we have all day to think about it," she said as she closed the cabinet. "Come on, let's go to work."

Both officers were quiet on the drive to the ferry landing where they would begin their day. They were both thinking of a solution to the dilemma.

Gayle was nowhere to be seen when they arrived to cross the river. She probably had a day off, thought Holden. Carrying their packs, they crossed the river to begin their day. It was pleasant visiting with the fishermen along the stream. Most were friendly and some asked questions about, "How do I go about catching these Sockeye Salmon?"

Holden always told them of the legal restrictions on how far the weight must be above the 'Russian River Fly', and the basics of catching a fish that ordinarily doesn't strike as other fishes do. It was a matter of getting the fly to hook the fish on the inside of the mouth where it would be a legal catch.

Goddard admired her patience with all fishermen and feared he would never be able to do this job with the same professionalism she had shown. He followed her downstream, assisting with fish counts on stringers and standing by as a backup if there should be belligerent fisherman. It seemed that even impatient fishermen allowed her to check them without confrontation.

It was still early in the day when they reached the usual spot they'd used to observe the bear's fishing hole. They sat on the same old log and opened the backpack for the thermos bottle and cups. The sun was high in the sky, and it was warm. Cooler weather was approaching, as indicated by the high cirrus clouds moving in from the south. They sat quietly, sipping coffee and watching the river. It was a peaceful scene. There were a few fishermen on the other side of the river and some onlookers looking to spot one of the brown bears fishing in the stream. None had appeared yet this morning.

Around noon a black bear with a small cub came to the river, but only watched the fishermen on the other side before moving on toward the hillside a mile east, where mushrooms were still available on shaded forest floor. Les and Betty watched as the bears moved back into the forest and disappeared from sight.

An hour later, Les was nearly asleep when a cow moose and her calf came to the river. They stood on the high bank and watched for a long while before walking to the water's edge and wading, then swimming to the highway side of the river. Heavy summer traffic on the highway made it difficult for the cow to take her calf across the roadway safely. She finally found a break between the cars and moved across the highway and up the steep embankment on the other side.

An occasional duck floated down the river, mostly Mergansers, a type of fish-eating duck. The hens each had a large following of chicks, some with twenty or more. They floated near shore looking for their main diet staple of small salmon, moving downstream.

Betty Holden marveled at the relaxing scenery. She was finding it difficult to sit and do nothing, but these peaceful interludes seldom lasted long. She reached inside her pack for a ham and cheese sandwich and a new cup of coffee. As she took out the Tupperware container she had stored a sandwich in, she heard a sudden, blood-curdling roar from inside the tree line. It immediately drew the attention of both officers.

Les reached to tap her on the arm and asked in a whisper, "What in the world was that? It sounded like a lion roaring."

She held her finger to her lips. She leaned over to whisper to her partner, "I've heard that in the past. I think there are two male brownies up there in the trees and they're about to have a fight. Just sit tight and don't say a word. The loser will be leaving after the fight, and he won't be in a good mood. I don't want him to see us. SHHH," she said.

Another roar. Only this time it was certain there was more than one animal making the sounds. The roaring sounds continued for more than two hours. Finally, it was quiet. Holden pulled her shotgun close to her side. As the officers watched the wooded area, they noticed movement in the trees. Soon, a brown bear with a very blond colored hide, came out of the woods. It stopped on the trail to look at the river, but finally continued downstream. It was easy to see this was the loser in the fight. A large patch of hide had been ripped from the center of his back to his left rear paw. The patch was nearly three inches wide and nearly two feet long. This was not a happy bear. Once the loser was out of sight all became quiet for another hour before the winner came to the river. His hide showed wet patches where he had been bitten during the melee. The winner was the 'big boy'.

The bear studied the fishing hole for several minutes before descending to the river's edge and wading out into the water. Onlookers on the highway side of the river had moved back from the water's edge, knowing this was not an animal to antagonize. The onlookers watched and photographed the huge bear while he caught and consumed his dinner.

After nearly an hour of catching and eating his salmon dinner, the bear climbed the steep bank and wandered back into the woods where he'd been fighting.

The two officers sat quietly for several minutes before Holden finally asked, "Well, have you had enough for one day?"

"Oh my gosh, I've never seen or heard anything like that. They sounded like two lions fighting. I can see why you were so cautious. That other bear would have taken on anything that caught his attention. He was not a happy camper when he left the woods." He held out his hands, "Look at me, I'm still shaking."

"I want you to remember this fight. The loser left town and the winner came down for bragging rights. I'm willing to bet the female bear is out there in the woods and that these males were fighting over her. Kinda like Saturday night at the strip club." Betty finally took a bite of her sandwich, which had still lain in the plastic box next to her shotgun. "Come on, let's go home and write our report. I've had enough excitement for one day."

"Well, at least we didn't have any hunters to check today," quipped Les.

"I'm happy to say," she replied with a smile, still chewing on her sandwich.

A half hour later they crossed the river on the ferry and tossed their packs in the backseat of her State truck.

At about this same time, in a home in the Muldoon section of Anchorage, three hunters were loading equipment into a pickup truck and hooking up the small boat and trailer to the hitch.

Burt Donnigan was directing the loading process. He asked Lou Phelps to go into the den and find enough food and supplies to last two days.

"There's bottles of water, canned meat, some pilot bread and powdered eggs and milk in the cupboard. Divide it up into the three backpacks and keep it light," said the leader.

"I thought we were starting early," mentioned Dave Forsythe.

"Yeah, I thought about that. But we've seen those Fish and Wildlife Troopers down there working all day. They seem to leave the river late in the afternoon and I thought if we went in late, they may have gone home. We stand a better chance of getting across the river without being seen by the law. We can find a place to sort of hide the boat in the brush along the riverbank across from Jim's Landing."

"That's good thinking, Burt," said Dave, asking, "Where's your rifle?"

"In the case next to my backpack. It's my lightweight .338. It has iron sights, but we agreed we wouldn't need a scope on this hunt. I'm also taking my .460 Smith in a holster on my hip as a backup. You might be well advised to carry something with you, too. If I go down, you may need to protect yourself," said Burt.

Lou spoke up, "Dave and I each taking our Ruger .44 Magnums. They're kinda heavy, but at close range are as effective as a rifle."

"Good thinking, guys. Now, let's get loaded and on the road. It's going to be late by the time we get to the river as it is. That's good for us, but it's going to make for an awfully long day. I only hope we find the bear tonight and not have to spend the night in the woods. Let's get going now." Then as an afterthought he asked, "Want to take any beer along for the drive down?"

"Maybe a sixpack," said Lou.

It was past midnight when they dropped the small boat in the water at Jim's Landing and loaded their equipment in the little craft. Burt and Dave climbed aboard the small boat with Burt at the oars. They drifted quite a distance downstream before they reached the other shore, aiding them in finding a place to conceal the boat.

Lou watched them from shore as they made their way across and out of sight on the other shore. It was decided he would take the truck and trailer to the trailhead on Skilak Road and hike down the trail to the river above the white-water rapids in the canyon. He'd hike down the trail to the river to take the pack, containing the bear hide and skull, up the trail to the truck while Burt and Dave would continue down the river, through the rapids and onto Skilak Lake. The small battery power motor was tied inside the boat to prevent it from falling out in case the boat capsized while negotiating the swift water of the canyon. Lou was to meet them at the upper Skilak Boat Landing on the lake.

He would be able to get a good night's sleep while the two hunters were searching the woods for an angry bear. He liked the idea. He drove the truck and trailer to the parking area at the landing to get some sleep and to await the arrival of the other two. Before he could leave, he had to wait for his partners to kill and skin the bear. That could be an all-night hunt. He found a picnic bench at the trail head and waited for the hunters. It was a good time to drink that last beer as he waited.

On the other side of the river the two hunters catnapped during the darkest part of the night, but at the first signs of daylight they were up and moving, slowly canvassing the woods near where the bear was last seen. They hunted all that day and until noon the following day before giving up the hunt. What they didn't know was the bear had followed the female up the hillside to a grassy area where they were grazing on lush, green fireweed leaves.

Late the second afternoon it was apparent they'd lost the bear, at least for now. They made a slow trip back to the boat and rowed it across the Kenai River. By the time they reached shore they were near the trailhead where Lou was still waiting.

They tossed a rope to Lou, who pulled the boat to dry land. They climbed out and asked for a bottle of water. "We couldn't find the stinking bear," said Dave, in disgust.

"How come?" asked a surprised Lou.

Burt took the water bottle from his lips to answer, "I don't know. We found his tracks in several places and then lost them in the brush. We looked everywhere we could get to, but never even smelled him. For some reason I think he left the river."

"What now?" asked Lou.

Burt turned to Dave Forsythe, "You have a choice, Dave. You can go with Lou and meet me at the landing, or you can come with me down the canyon, just for the ride."

It took only a few seconds for him to decide, "I guess I'll go downriver with you. You may need some help and, if I go with Lou, I'll have to listen to him for hours. I'll just go with you." The three men laughed.

It took several hours to cross the lake after the long and bumpy trip through the white waters of the canyon. Once on the open waters of the lake, using the electric motor, the ride was smooth and quiet. Dave napped for a while. Upon awakening he asked, "Do you want to take a nap and let me drive for a while?"

"Yeah, I think I will. Can you see that tall hill on the point over there?" he asked while pointing in the direction of the far shore. "Just head that way and the landing is on the other side. Wake me when we get close."

In just moments he was asleep.

CHAPTER 15

At her usual 0500 arrival time, Holden entered the office to find Ted Wilson already at his desk. He heard her enter and called for her to come into his office.

She gave him a small wave of her hand as she entered, "Good morning, Boss," she said in a cheery tone.

"Same to you, Holden. I heard you had an exciting afternoon on the river yesterday." He was smiling broadly.

"It sure was. Bears, moose, bears fighting in the woods. It doesn't get much better than that."

"How did Les react to all the commotion?" he asked.

"You know, I was surprised. As green as he is about bears, he's learning quickly and catches on fast. He's a smart young man, on top of being ambitious and having a lot of savvy about animals. He's also a quick study. I never have to tell him anything a second time. I like this kid." Betty was sincere in her assessment of the summer hire officer.

"Did you have any contact with the hunters?" he asked.

"No. And I thought it was strange. I would have guessed they'd come back as soon as possible to get another chance at that trophy bear. Guess I was wrong this time," she shrugged her shoulders.

"It may seem like a waste of time, but I want the two of you to go back again today. Safety for the public is my justification for doing that. Safety for the bear is also a concern for me. I'm sure your presence on the riverbank is keeping the fishermen more honest, so being there does have a useful purpose besides keeping an eye on the bear. Stick with it a few more days or until the bear leaves the river. Once he goes back to the mountains, I can find him with an air search. As an added bonus, I see you're writing a number of licenses and over-limit citations. Stay with it, Holden," he said with a smile and small wave of his hand to tell her they were through for now.

Les was waiting in her office when she entered. "Good morning," he said in a pleasant voice. "Are you going to show me some more bear fights today?"

She snickered and said, "Perhaps, but I want it to be a surprise. Are you ready to go?"

"Yup," he said, picking up his insulated coffee cup.

As usual, it took almost an hour to reach the ferry crossing where Gayle was sitting in her truck. She waved at the officers as they drove into the parking area.

"Good morning, Gayle," greeted Betty as she climbed out of the truck. "Did you enjoy your day off?"

Gayle laughed, "Sure did, if you can enjoy doing laundry and mopping floors. How was your day without me as a backup?"

"Oh wow, Gayle. You should've been here. The big bear had a challenger come to the neighborhood and they had one heck of a fight. The newcomer left with a sizable chunk of hide ripped loose from his back down his left hind leg. He was in a bad mood when he left the fishing hole."

"What's on your menu for today," asked Gayle.

"Same old, same old," replied Betty. "We'll be checking licenses and counting stringers today. We hope to see the big bear later at the fishing hole. Is there anything special we need to be on the lookout for?"

"I don't know of anything else, but if you're near the ferry landing around noon, I'll buy you and your partner some lunch up at Sunrise."

"I can't promise, but I'll try to get back here by then. Thanks, Gayle," she said, picking up her backpack from the back seat of the truck, pulling the straps onto her shoulders. She turned to Les, "Come on, Partner, time to go to work."

They were nearly back down to the bear's fishing hole when a non-resident fisherman stopped her to ask a question. "Hi, there. I know you're busy, but I'm from New Jersey and I was here yesterday when those bears were fighting back there in the trees. I've never heard anything like that. Does that sort of thing happen often up here in Alaska?"

"Not often, but it does happen. It seldom happens near where there are a lot of people. It's my guess they were fighting over the female we saw here the day before. As a rule, the loser leaves the area, but if I were you, I'd keep my eyes open." Holden offered the hint as a caution to the tourist. "After all, we can't have someone from New Jersey getting injured by one of our bears." She was smiling at the newcomer.

The officers were near the fishing hole. "How about we just go to our hiding spot and sit for a while?" she asked.

"Are you planning to meet Gayle for lunch?" asked Les.

"I doubt it. It's a long way to the ferry landing and a waste of time. If we sit here, we can watch for illegal fishing and wait for the big bear to show himself." Betty didn't like sitting and watching any better than young Les Goddard.

An hour into the wait, Holden's radio delivered a message. It was Gayle. "Holden, come up to the ferry landing. A fisherman has fallen in the river with a pack on his back and is being swept downstream. He doesn't appear to be able to swim, at least with the heavy pack on his shoulders. I need some help."

"We'll be right there. Let me know if he gets out of the water.?"

"Roger that," replied Gayle.

Holden and her partner jogged up the trail, scanning the river for any sign of the fallen fisherman. Halfway to the landing she saw a backpack sinking in the river. She pointed to the spot to show Les. He immediately dropped his pack, ran down the steep, rocky bank and jumped into the icy water. Swimming as quickly as he could to reach the nearly submerged backpack, he grasped the pack and pulled it around to bring the fisherman to the surface. He appeared unconscious and not breathing.

On shore, Betty saw Les struggling with the heavy fisherman. She had a spool of small rope in her pack and quickly opened it. She tossed the roll of rope down the trail, picked up a rock and tied it to the end of the rope. Swinging it over her head to build momentum, she gave it a fling in the direction of Les and his victim.

Les was able to grasp the small rope tightly while Betty put her weight into pulling the two men to shore. As he neared shore and regained his footing, Les was able to drag the fisherman onto land. He was pulling the man's pack from his shoulders as Betty reached the water's edge to assist. Together, they managed to get the pack from his shoulders and begin CPR.

Within seconds the fisherman began to spew river water from his mouth and to cough and choke. Les rolled the man onto his right side to allow to water to escape more easily. The man began to gag and cough and took a long breath of air. Suddenly he opened his eyes and panicked. Les held his shoulders tightly to calm the man.

It was several minutes before the man could speak, "Thank you," he said choking and coughing as he spoke.

Above them on the high riverbank, Gayle was calling for an ambulance on her radio. The Cooper Landing Volunteer Fire Department was responding to the call.

The man was sitting up now, though bent forward and still coughing up water. It took a little time for the EMT crew of two to cross the river at the ferry and run while carrying a lightweight stretcher with them. One medic carried the small stretcher as the other carried the medical kit. It was an awkward rescue, but the medics took to the task of being sure the man was no longer in distress. They sat on the riverbank with him and monitored his pulse and breathing. His friends had gathered on the high bank above the water and asked a lot of questions Gayle was unable to answer. Les and Betty climbed the high bank from the water to assist their fellow officer with the crowd gathered there.

The group were friends from Oregon. They had rented a motorhome in Anchorage and were spending the week in the Russian River Campground where only last week there'd been a man killed at night by a brown bear. The four friends of the man who had fallen into the river were concerned for the well-being of their friend.

Les carried the man's pack to the top of the high bank, about 25 feet above the water level. The friends asked if they would take possession of the backpack. It took several minutes to get the names and addresses of all the friends, but it was obvious they were all in the same party.

By now, the medics had the victim on his feet, walking him slowly in small circles on the gavel of the riverbed. They aided his climb up the steep bank to the top, where his friends were waiting. Once again, the medics made the man sit on the ground where they checked his heartbeat and blood pressure. He seemed to be doing well, but they continued to monitor him for several more minutes before releasing him.

Les walked back to the ferry and crossed with them to sit in the truck in an attempt to get dry and warm. A half hour later Betty and Gayle followed.

"It looks like we'll have trouble with Old Les here wanting to play in the water all the time," Betty was making a joke with Gayle. The lady officers laughed, but Les couldn't find any humor in it. He was still very cold and very wet. Betty turned to Gayle, "Is that invitation for lunch still open?" she asked.

"You bet, I'll buy lunch for anyone who saves one of my fishermen," she said, laughing at her own joke.

After reporting the incident to Sergeant Wilson, they drove to the Sunrise Inn for a welcome lunch and short rest before resuming their routine.

After lunch they thanked Gayle and returned to foot patrol of the far side of the river. They walked back down to the bear's fishing hole and found their seat on the old log to wait for any bears to arrive at the fishing grounds.

Finally dry and warm, Les asked, "Is it always like this? I mean, is it always boring for a while and then screaming with excitement the next moment?"

Holden chuckled, "That's the way life is in all law enforcement. Hopefully your days are filled with more boredom than excitement. I think you may have learned that lesson today, but I also think you feel how satisfying it is to save someone's life. For what it's worth, I admired the way you didn't stop to think about it. You just jumped into the water to help that man. It shows that you have guts, young man."

Les chuckled, "To be honest, I never even thought about it. I just saw him in trouble and dropped my pack to help him. I had forgotten just how cold the water was until I dove into it."

Holden smiled and nodded. The officers sat in the sunshine and waited for the bears to appear, but they didn't show themselves. By late afternoon, they decided it was time to return to the office to write reports on the activities of the afternoon. Les slept most of the way back to the office. She told him to go home and get some rest while she finished the official report.

In the office, Betty stopped to visit with the Sergeant, "Can I talk with you a minute?" she asked.

"Sure, come on in and have a seat." He pointed at the chair on the other side of his desk. "I heard you two had another exciting day. What happened? I heard the stuff on the radio, but what really happened?"

"Glad you asked, Sarge. I want to ask you to recommend Les for a commendation. We got a radio call that someone had fallen in the water and was swept downstream. We were halfway back to the ferry when we saw the man float by. He was underwater and not moving his arms. Les stripped off his backpack and ran down the embankment, jumped into the water and got the man's head above water. I threw him a line and helped him get to the riverbank. Gayle called the medics and we tried to do rescue CPR on the victim. We got him breathing again and he was spitting out water from his lungs. Les Goddard is a man of action. This is the second time I've seen him in the river. I don't want to sound like he's reckless, but he meets any challenge without fear. I really like this young man."

Ted leaned back in his desk chair, removed his cap and scratched his head. "I heard about him jumping in the river. Write your report and I'll see what I can do about the commendation. I'll use your report as a memo to the Colonel. I agree, he's going to make a good officer someday."

CHAPTER 16

The following morning, after she finished her breakfast and put on her uniform, she was gathering her coffee and strapping on her duty weapon when the phone rang. She looked at her watch. It read 0430. She wondered who'd be calling at this hour. She picked up the receiver. "Hello," she answered.

"Betty, its Ted Wilson. I'm in the office. I need to see you when you get here. Come into my office."

"OK, Sarge, I'm just leaving the house. Should be there in about ten minutes." She hung up the phone, wondering what had happened to warrant this early morning call.

Inside the office building she went directly to the Sergeant's office, "What's going on, Boss?" she asked.

"I had an early morning call from the Trooper working the Cooper Landing area. He told me he had just seen a pickup truck towing a small aluminum boat and followed it to Jim's Landing. He checked out the license plate of the truck. It's registered to Burt Donnigan. He said there were three men in the truck. They backed the boat trailer into the water at the ramp in the landing. He called me to ask what action to take. I told him to leave them alone and I'd have you check it out when you get up there. That's what I want you to do."

"It sounds like they may be going after the bear again." she commented.

"At this point we don't know what they're doing, but I want you to check it out. I also want you to use extreme caution. I think these men could get dangerous, so be careful," warned the Sergeant.

"I'll check them out on our way to the ferry landing. I'll let you know what we find."

She was waiting in her truck when Les arrived. She rolled down her window and called to him to bring his shotgun.

He pulled his backpack from the back seat of his vehicle. Reaching back into the rear seat, he grabbed his shotgun, walked to Betty's truck and put the pack and the gun on the rear seat. As he climbed into the front seat he asked, "What's going on, Partner?"

She checked traffic and made a quick turn onto the main road. There wasn't much traffic on the streets at this time of day, but she was being cautious anyway. "OK," she said, as she pressed hard on the throttle. "The hunters were seen late last night at Jim's Landing. We were ordered to check them out, just to see what they're up to."

It was late-night, but the summer sky was more like dusk than night. The three men unloaded the boat. Donnigan and Forsythe climbed aboard to row the boat to the other side of the river. Lou Phelps watched them as they crossed, stashing the boat in a clump of brush nearly a half mile downstream. Phelps went back to the truck and towed the little trailer out of the water. He drove up Skilak Loop Road to park at the canyon trailhead, and again slept on the picnic table at the river's edge.

When Holden reached the Skilak Loop turn she drove into Jim's Landing campground to search for the truck. It was nowhere to be seen. She sat for a while staring at the river. Minutes later she turned to Goddard. "You know? These hunters were here before. I suspect the truck is still in the area somewhere. Let's check a couple of parking lots. There's a trailhead and parking up the road here about two miles. Let's check that one out first."

Les only nodded.

"Bingo!" she exclaimed as they neared the parking area. "Let's check the truck out and give Sarge a call on the radio."

They looked through the windows to see if there was any hunting gear inside. There wasn't anything left inside the pickup. She called Sergeant Wilson to report finding the truck.

Wilson listened and said, "Good work Holden. Now go on about your other duties and keep your eyes open for the hunters, but don't wander off into the woods to look for them. I have another officer patrolling both of Skilak Lake's landings. I'll have him keep an eye on the truck up there. Try to keep Goddard out of the river today."

With that he signed off the radio. Betty and Les laughed at the sergeant's footnote.

They'd been doing patrol most of the day and were having a sandwich at their favorite secret spot when Holden's radio beeped.

"Holden," she answered.

"Sergeant Wilson," said the voice on the other end. "We have a situation out near you. It looks like those hunters ran into trouble and are calling for help. It was someone else who called, but they said one of the hunters needed an ambulance. I want you to go up to the canyon trailhead and check it out. These are still dangerous men and I want you to use caution when you contact them."

"Got it, Boss. Les and I are leaving right now. We're downstream and it will take a while to get to the ferry. We're on our way," reported Holden.

"What do you think happened, Betty?" asked Goddard.

"I don't know, but it could be anything. Perhaps they just fell down and accidentally shot a partner, or the bear could have chewed one of them up. It could be any one of a dozen things. Let's go find out what really happened. They shouldn't have been there, so for them to call us, it must be serious."

Twenty minutes later they pulled into the trailhead parking area. "Bring your shotgun and keep me covered while we find out what happened," said Betty as she checked her sidearm and shotgun.

The officers hiked down the trail to the riverside where there was a small crowd gathered. An injured man was lying on the picnic table, covered with a blanket from somewhere, maybe from one of the spectators. The crowd parted to allow the officers to get to the wounded man. Two men were attempting to stem the flow of blood from the man on the table.

"Mr. Donnigan, what happened?" she asked.

"It's David! He was attacked by a bear on the other side of the river," explained Donnigan.

"The ambulance is on its way and should be here any minute. What can we do to help?" she asked.

Donnigan was tearful now, "We can't get the bleeding stopped," he said, nearly sobbing.

She pulled off her pack and reached inside for the medical kit. She found a stack of 4x4 gauze pads and began applying pressure to slow the bleeding. She ordered Donnigan and his other partner to hold the pads tightly. She applied several more pads and had the men hold those also.

The man on the table was unconscious but moaning in pain. Some of the wounds had pierced his abdomen and that couldn't be covered with a pad. She attempted to make a larger gauze pad with bandaging material, but it didn't stop the bleeding. It did slow the bleeding quite a lot. She took a belt from one of the people nearby and made a tourniquet which she wrapped tightly around the victim. This slowed the bleeding a great deal. As she stepped back to assess the injuries, she heard someone in the crowd say the medics had arrived. There were four of them. She stepped aside to allow the EMTs to do their job.

She went to the river to wash the blood from her hands and arms. Donnigan did the same. Les stood back a little to keep a clear shot between himself and the two at the river's edge.

The medics had strapped an IV bag to his arm and were loading him into the basket-style stretcher they had carried down the trail.

The team leader called out to Holden, "Officer Holden," when she looked up, he continued. "We need to get his man to the hospital right now. We'll be taking him to Soldotna. We don't have a helicopter available right now, so we'll be driving him to town."

"OK, I'll be there later to check on him. Call Ted Wilson and let him know what's going on. I'll be along soon," Holden barked the orders with authority.

A sobbing Donnigan was now asking, "Is he going to be alright?"

"I don't know, but I want you and your other partner to walk back to the truck with me. I'll need some information for my report. What were the two of you doing over on the other side of the river anyway?" she asked.

"Fishing for Sockeye," he lied.

Holden looked at Goddard and said, "Bring up the rear, Les."

Les understood what he was asked to do and followed the several people now climbing the trail back to the road and parking area.

Following the group to the ambulance took almost half an hour. When they arrived at the parking lot, they immediately replaced the bag of fluids being poured into his arm. Les and Betty stood by until the ambulance left the parking area, red lights and sirens clearing traffic ahead.

Once the injured man was on the way to the hospital, Betty Holden turned to Donnigan and Lou Phelps. "OK, you two. No more fairy tales. What were you doing on the other side of the river?" she asked in an official voice.

"I told you, we were fishing," Donnigan repeated.

"Without a fishing rod or a fly? Come on Burt, you're going to have to do better than that," she said calmly.

Donnigan hung his head for a moment, then became defiant. "Look, I told you we were fishing. I ain't saying nothing else until I talk with my lawyer."

"I guess you leave me no choice, Burt. I am arresting you and your partner here, for illegally hunting brown bears in a closed area. Turn around while I put the cuffs on you." She took the handcuffs from her belt and turned to Les, "Put your cuffs on Burt's partner," she said.

Burt Donnigan made a motion like he wanted to resist arrest. Les jabbed his ribs with the barrel of the shotgun. He took the hint and placed his hands behind his back for Betty to place cuffs on his wrists.

Les took the backpacks from the back seat and placed them in the bed of the truck. After Donnigan and Phelps were strapped into the rear seat, Les handed his shotgun to Betty to store in the front seat with her as she drove. Les would remain in the rear seat with the two prisoners.

Once on the road, Betty used her radio to report to Sergeant Wilson. She told her boss the victim was in the ambulance on the way to the hospital and that the other two hunting partners had been arrested and were on the way to Wildwood Pretrial Facility.

"Let me know when you get them booked in. I want to see you in the office as soon as possible," said Wilson.

It seemed like an exceptionally long drive to the jail facility in Kenai, taking more than an hour. She signed the remand forms and told the guard to allow them to contact their lawyer as soon as they were finished with the booking process.

Les was now in the front seat with his partner, "Man, that was tense," he said.

"They didn't give us an alternative. They refused to cooperate. I'll bet if we go out to where they had the attack, we could find their rifles. The Sarge may send someone else to look for the attack

site and have a look around. I hope he does. I'm
getting ready for dinner and some hot food for a
change,"

"I'd like you to know how much I admire
the way you handled these men. You're right
about them being dangerous. They were pretty set
on getting that bear. I guess I have a lot to learn
about these situations. I tend to believe what
people tell me. I need to learn that it doesn't
always work that way. I learned a lot today.
Thanks for the lessons." It was a grateful Les
Goddard speaking in appreciation of the
instruction.

In the office the officers went to see the
Sergeant. He asked for an oral report and Holden
gave him the entire incident. "I still have no word
on the condition of the injured man. Have you
heard?"

"No, I haven't. I'll call the hospital right
now. We may need to send a guard over there to
guard him if he's a prisoner."

Wilson dialed the hospital emergency room
desk to inquire about the condition of the victim of
the bear attack. The girl at the desk recognized
Ted Wilson's voice.

"They're still working on him, Sergeant.
He's in surgery right now. I can have the doctor
call you as soon as they take him to recovery, if
you'd like," she offered.

"Yes, I think that would be important. He
may be under arrest. We may need to send

someone to guard him as a prisoner. He hasn't been booked into jail yet, so the Troopers are going to need to supply a guard." Wilson hung up the telephone and returned his attention to his officers. "You two did an excellent job out there today. The medics called and said they thought you probably saved this man's life with your quick actions and improvising the tourniquet the way you did. Good work. Both of you. Now write up your report and go home. I'll send a trooper to look for the attack site. There may be some evidence at the site," Wilson was making a note on his desk as the officers went to Betty's office.

"They may find some rifles at the site. Which reminds me, we need to tag those handguns we took when we arrested Donnigan and Phelps."

"I'll bring them to the office and tag them while you write the rest of the report," offered Goddard.

CHAPTER 17

Les Goddard brought the handguns to the office and began to put evidence tags on each of them. Betty Holden was working at her desk writing the report of the incident. When Goddard finished his chore, she told him to go home and be ready to start again with her tomorrow. She continued to work on the report for another hour.

When she had proof-read the final draft, she stopped for the day and went home for a hot shower and some hot food. She was totally exhausted. It had been a tense and physically draining day. After dinner and a shower she collapsed into bed and slept without waking until the alarm awakened her at 0430. She rolled over to turn off the alarm and stretched her aching body.

"I'm getting too old for this kind of work," she thought to herself as she stood and limbered her muscles with some stretching exercises. She was eighteen years on the force and loved every minute of her duty, but the tension of the situation coupled with the physical strength used the day before had tested her nearly to the limits of her aging ability.

After breakfast, with her thermos bottle filled, she drove to the office to meet Les. He was sitting in his vehicle listening to the radio when she arrived. She stopped alongside his rig and waited for him to load his pack into the rear seat.

"I guess I'll never have to be reminded to take my shotgun with me after yesterday's activity," he joked as he closed the door and settled into the passenger seat. "Good morning, Officer Holden," he offered in a friendly tone.

"And good morning to you, too," she replied. "Are you ready for a walk in the woods?"

"Yes, of course." He looked her in the eye and said, "I shouldn't admit this, but when I got home and had time to think about it, I had a lot of fun yesterday. I admit I had no idea what to do next, but when it was over, I'd learned a lot and that I liked the excitement and challenges of the entire day. Thank you for letting me be a part of the real action and not just having me stand by and watch."

"You did a great job out there, Les. You stayed back and stood watch and stepped in to help when it was needed. That showed a great deal of common sense. The only caution I can offer about it is, don't let the excitement rule your judgement. Some officers tend to create situations just for the excitement they get. Try to avoid that and you'll be a good officer and the public will be more willing to give you a hand when you need it."

"I'll try to remember that for the future. Again, I thank you for the chance to be a part of the action." Les was smiling broadly.

"Well, Partner," she said as she put the truck in gear, "Here we go again. We've been ordered to go into the woods and find the attack site. Sarge

thinks we could find a rifle or two out there. I
have to caution you; we could also find a terribly
angry bear." She giggled, "Are you ready for more
excitement?"

An hour later they were in the parking area
on the ferry landing drinking coffee when Gayle
parked alongside them.

"Hi, guys. What's on the to-do list today?"
she asked.

"We're ordered to find the attack site and
have a look around. I think we'll just cross on the
ferry and have a leisurely stroll downriver for
about five miles, saunter into the woods and visit
with the big old brown bear that lives there. It
should be fun. Wanna come along?" Holden was
making light of her assignment, but deep down she
knew just how dangerous this could become.

"Gee, I wish I could. But I have to stick
around here and keep an eye on the tourists. You
can leave Les with me if you want. Just in case
another fisherman falls in the river," she chuckled.

"Sorry, I can't do that. He's my backup in
case the big bear wants to argue about who owns
the woods." Now they were all laughing.

Minutes later the ferry returned and the
officers crossed to the others side of the Kenai
River. They slipped their packs on their backs and
began the long walk to the woods below the bear's
fishing hole. As they neared the area where the
trail entered the woods, Betty said, "I hope you

brought your camera today, just in case we find the area of the attack."

"It's in my pack," he said as he followed her down the trail.

The walk went quickly until they reached the woods. They were forced to slow the pace to watch for bears. It was another mile and a half before they came across the footprints of Donnigan and his partner. They were able to follow the tracks until they left the main bear trail. It was difficult, but they were able to follow the men's path through the broken wild parsnip and tall grass to where there was a large, flattened patch of vegetation.

"Better get out your camera, Les. This looks like the spot of the attack." They began to search the flattened vegetation. They soon found a large spattering of blood on the broad leaves. Les snapped photos of anything he thought was important. They found a large pool of drying blood.

"This must be where the bear took Forsythe down," she noted. "Look around in the tall weeds for a rifle or two."

The search continued as the officers looked for any evidence. They found some torn clothing soaked in blood on one side of the thirty-foot circle of flattened vegetation. At the edge of the circle, under a large parsnip leaf, she saw the end of a gunstock. She had Les photograph the spot and the gun before retrieving it.

"Nice rifle," said Betty as she inspected the weapon and cleared the chamber. She leaned it against a small tree and continued to search. The vegetation was torn to bare ground in one small area.

"This could be where the two men were attacked and where Donnigan attempted to protect Forsythe. It looks like the bear disarmed Burt and the bear tried to kill David."

Les was on the other side of the small area when he called to his partner, "Hey Holden, come over here," he said. "Look at this."

She walked to the spot and Les pointed to a patch of bare ground at the edge of the flattened circle. "Old Burt may have crawled into the vegetation here to escape the bear while he was chewing up Forsythe."

Betty could see where there were drag marks, like the toes of shoes scraping soft ground. "I think you're right. Get some pictures of that, will you Les?"

He snapped several pictures while Betty picked up a broken limb to hold back the vegetation. The drag marks continued for almost ten yards into the parsnips and grass. Where the marks ended there were boot prints.

"The bear must have gone away and Burt stood up here." She turned to look around the area.

"Look over that way, Les. I can see where the bear attacked Forsythe. He must have finished chewing on the man and wandered off into the woods. Let's see if we can find any tracks to indicate which direction he went."

After more than half an hour they found nothing more. "I guess we've done as much as we can here, Partner. Let's get out of these woods. I'll get the rifle and meet you at the trail." She was relieved to be able to go without having an encounter of their own with this bear.

They walked back up the trail to where they'd previously sat to watch the bears.

"It's early yet, we could just sit here and eat our lunch while we watch the river," she said, placing the rifle against the log they used for a seat.

After eating his lunch, Les got his camera from his pack and reviewed the photos he'd taken. They were clear digital pictures disclosing every detail of the attack. He showed the pictures to Betty. She marveled at the quality she saw.

After lunch, they watched the fishing hole for almost an hour before deciding to go back to the office.

When they arrived at the office, Betty went directly to her desk to draft a report while Les made an evidence tag for the rifle and locked it in the evidence locker. They were just finishing when Ted Wilson came back to the office.

"How'd you do?" he asked.

Betty called Les to the office. "Show the Sarge your pictures, Les."

He placed the camera on the desk and began to show the pictures and explained what each one was a picture of. The Sergeant was impressed beyond words.

"Those photos are really great. Can we get prints made of each of those?" he asked.

"Sure, Sarge, no problem. I'll have prints for you this afternoon. Do you want an extra copy of each?" asked Goddard.

"That would be wonderful, Les. We can't just take them to Walgreens to be printed. Can you do this yourself?" asked the Sergeant.

"Oh, sure. I have a printer and can make prints on full sheets of photo paper. I'll have them for you by morning," Les volunteered.

"I'll have the office pay you for the paper and ink," noted the Sergeant. "Did you sight the bear?" he asked.

"No, but as dense as the foliage is out there, he could have been watching us all the time. I doubt he was doing that, but we never saw him. Have you heard from the hospital about David Forsythe or his condition?" she asked.

"No, but it's on my list of things to do today. The Trooper office has a man on his door, a contract guard. He can't run anywhere for a while, but he's a prisoner and regs say we have to put a guard on the door." Wilson was shaking his head, "I have an appointment with the DA tomorrow morning to discuss possible charges against Donnigan and Phelps. We'll need to check records to see if the rifle is registered to Burt, but I think his being there will be enough proof for any jury." Ted Wilson stood to return to his own office. "You did good, guys," he said as he left the office.

Les looked at his partner, "You know, I owe you a meal or two. How about we go to Froso's for dinner before we go home?" he asked.

"Are you sure you want to do that?" she asked.

"You bet. I owe you more than a dinner." He laughed, "If you weren't in uniform, I'd buy you a glass of wine to go with it."

"Give me time to stop at the house and I'll drink it. It sounds like a good idea tonight."

"I'll meet you at Froso's restaurant in a half hour," he said as he stood to leave.

"I'll be there. And thanks, Les." She replied.

After they left the office, Ted Wilson was at his desk when his phone rang. It was Burt Donnigan at the jail.

"Sergeant Wilson, this is Burt Donnigan and my lawyer told me I should call you. Have you heard any word about David Forsythe?" he asked.

"No, I haven't. I intend to call the hospital in a little while. I'll send word back to you about his condition if there's any word. Is that what you wanted to ask?" uttered Wilson.

"No. Well, yes. But my lawyer said I should call you and offer to cooperate. I just wanted to know about David," explained Donnigan.

"Are you offering to cooperate in this investigation?" asked Wilson.

"I guess I should. The whole thing was my idea. Phelps and Forsythe were just helping me out. They like to hunt and I take them on guided hunts sometimes to repay them for helping me. I want you to know I'm not usually a poacher, but I saw this bear and became obsessed with taking the largest bear ever sighted on the Kenai Peninsula. I had to have it." He paused a few seconds, "But the cost has been far too high. I don't want to lose a good friend over a bear hide." There was a great sadness in his voice.

"Would it be OK with you if I sent an officer to the jail and get your recorded statement?" asked Wilson.

"I ain't goin' nowhere," said Donnigan, "I'll be here."

CHAPTER 18

The following morning, Wilson had given Holden and Goddard the day off. Sergeant Joe Derks was sent to the Kenai jail to interview Burt Donnigan. Derks was an experienced officer and an excellent interviewer. He locked his weapon in the gun safe box and entered the facility. He asked to see Donnigan in the attorney visiting room. Burt was brought to the front, without handcuffs or chains because he wasn't considered a dangerous person. He was sitting in the attorney room when Derks was told he could go inside.

Burt was sitting in a chair, head bowed, looking at the floor when Derks entered. "Hello there, Mr. Donnigan," began Derks. "I'm Sergeant Derks and was asked by Sergeant Wilson to come to Kenai to speak with you."

"Howdy, Sergeant. I'm Burt. Just plain Burt. Yeah, I talked with Wilson yesterday. I told him I'd cooperate with him. He said he'd send someone over today."

"Yes, that's correct. Do you have any objections to speaking into a recorder? It saves me a lot of writing and wasting our time together" asked Derks.

"No, do what you gotta do. My lawyer told me to cooperate, and I will. But before we start, can you tell me how David Forsythe is doing?"

"I talked with his doctor on my way over here. He told me your friend is still in critical condition, but his vital signs improved overnight. They're keeping him sedated because of the pain and the extent of his injuries. The doctor said he was in for a long hospital stay and a long session of physical rehab in the days to come." Derks was being as tactful as possible and tried not to be as graphic as the doctor had been.

Derks took a small recorder from his pocket and placed it on the table. He asked Donnigan to give his name and date of birth as an identifier on the tape. He also identified himself by name and badge number.

"Mr. Donnigan…."

He was interrupted by Donnigan, "Please, just call me Burt."

"Alright, Burt. I would like to begin with your previous arrest. You claimed at that time you were fishing and were attacked by the bear. Is that still your statement?"

Burt looked at the floor. "No, we were out there looking for the bear. We had seen him, and I went sorta crazy about it. He's the largest brown bear I have ever seen or heard of down here on the Kenai. That didn't go well, and Officer Holden and her partner caught us. She took our weapons and wrote us each a ticket. We went to court and got a fine. Lost our hunting privileges and our rifles."

"The lawyer you have now, is he the same one?" asked Derks.

"Yeah, he is," Burt replied.

"OK Burt. Let's talk about this added charge. I'm told you and your partners came down to the Kenai Peninsula for the purpose of killing this large brown bear. Is that correct?"

"Yeah, we put all the gear together and hooked up my little boat. We drove down here and planned to cross the river and go after the bear. We crossed the river and hunted all day until it got too late. We found a place to get some rest and started again the next day. Lou was waiting at the trail at the head of the canyon above the rapids. He was to take the hide to the truck while David and I went down the canyon, through the rapids and cross the lake to the upper Skilak Landing.

We didn't come out the first night but went back into the woods to look for the bear. It took a while, but we spotted a bear. It wasn't the big one. It looked like a small female. We were being quiet and watching the small blond bear when the big male came after us. He was close and we smelled him before we saw him. We turned around on the trail and saw him charging.

I pulled up my gun to shoot, but he hit me with his head as he ran by and attacked David. I couldn't find my rifle and crawled into the underbrush to hide. The bear kept biting and slapping poor old David with his claws. I was crying because I couldn't help my friend. I looked for the rifle when the bear left the area, but I couldn't find it. David was bleeding something awful, so I carried him to the river, put him in the boat and crossed. I went downstream to where Lou was waiting, hoping to get some help for David. Lou had been sleeping on the picnic table and helped me put David on it. There were a couple of fishermen there that saw David was injured so they offered to help.

That's when Officer Holden showed up and took over. Thank God, she knew what to do and stopped most of the bleeding. If David makes it, it'll be because of Officer Holden giving him the immediate care he needed. We tried to stop the bleeding, but we didn't have any luck. That Officer Holden did something we never thought of and made a thick pad she held in place with a fisherman's belt. His belly had been ripped open and his guts hanging out. She stuffed them back inside and put the pad over it and held it in place with that fisherman's belt."

Donnigan was sobbing and staring at the floor by the time he finished his answer. "Would you like something to drink, Burt?" asked Derks.

The Sergeant picked up the phone and punched intercom, "Is it possible to get a Coke or something for Mr. Donnigan?" he asked.

Moments later the door opened, and the guard handed Derks a large paper cup with what looked like Coca Cola filling it to the rim. He took the cup and handed it to Burt, who drank half the cupful with one continuous swallow.

"Thanks," he said, setting the cup on the desk.

"You're welcome. For what it's worth, we've been keeping tabs on the big bear since he moved into a populated area. I don't know if you'd heard, but a camper was killed at the Russian River Campground a few days ago. He was killed by a sow and cub without any apparent provocation." Derks related the condensed version of the story.

"I just want you to know I'm done with this bear. I can't believe how obsessed I had become over this bear. I don't know how I'll feel if David doesn't make it."

"Can you think of any other things you could have missed?" asked Derks.

Donnigan took another long drink of his Coke and thought for a moment. "No, I can't think of anything. But if I do, I'll call you."

"OK, then, Burt. I'll go back to the office. I appreciate your being honest with me." He picked up his recorder and returned it to his pocket and called for the guard to come take Donnigan back to his dorm.

Later at the office he had a long conference with Ted Wilson. Ted listened to the recording and admitted he couldn't think of anything Derks had missed.

Ted took off his cap to scratch his head, put it back on his head and gave orders to Sergeant Derks, "Give this recording to the secretary to be typed up. I gave Holden and Goddard a day off to rest. They've been spending long days up at

Russian River and need some time off. The bear is still a concern. If we don't see him at the fishing hole for a couple of days, I'm going to do an aerial surveillance flight in the area below the fishing hole, on the hillsides near the white-water canyon. I have a problem sending someone out to eliminate this bear, since the attack on humans was actually provoked."

"I'd sure like to be in the back seat when you do that flight, Sarge," said Derks.

"I'll try to let you know when," said Wilson.

"OK, Ted. I have a lot of work of my own to catch up on. I'll give the recording to the secretary and go back to my office. Thanks for allowing me to help out." He gave a small salute and left the office.

It was late, almost eight o'clock the following morning, when Betty Holden met Ted Wilson in his office. "Good morning, Boss. What's going on for us today?"

"Glad you're here, Betty. Yesterday I had Sergeant Derks go to the jail to do an interview with Donnigan. He did a respectable job and Old Burt cooperated all the way. He's having a lot of remorse about his friend getting injured by the bear. It's changed his entire outlook on the situation."

"How's Forsythe doing? Have you heard?" she asked.

Wilson checked the time, "I was about to call the hospital to ask that very question. Have a seat and I'll put the call on speaker."

Holden sat across from her boss and listened.

A nurse answered and asked Wilson to hold while she put him through to the attending physician. There was a long pause until the doctor picked up the phone, "Hello, Sergeant, this is Doctor Stafford, attending physician for Mr. Forsythe. What can I do for you this morning?"

"I was just checking on the condition of Mr. Forsythe. What can you tell me this morning?" Betty was listening to the conversation from across the desk.

"We still have him sedated. His vitals improved somewhat, during the night. He has another surgery scheduled for this morning. We're going to attempt to do a better fix on the damage to his intestines. Yesterday we only tried to stop the bleeding and sew up the cuts to the various parts of his body. He was cut up horrifically. I'm surprised he made it to the hospital. I heard one of your officers jury-rigged the pressure wrap to stop the hemorrhaging. I think that action saved his life. Give that officer an extra cup of coffee when you see him." Said the doctor.

"As a matter of fact, that officer is sitting in my office right now listening to our conversation. She's the officer you're speaking about. Officer Betty Holden."

"Well, thank you for your quick thinking. He was about out of blood by the time we saw him here at the hospital. Good job Officer Holden."

"Thank you, Sir. I just used basic first aid skills. I'm glad it helped."

"In any case, you saved a life without a doubt. Sergeant, give this lady a peppermint stick. She saved a life."   Stafford paused a moment, "I have to go now. We're about to take Mr. Forsythe to surgery. I'll try to call later to let you know how this surgery went."

Wilson hung up the phone and looked across the desk, smiling. "Everyone seems to think you were the hero of the day on this one," he said. "For what it's worth, I think so, too."

"Thanks, Boss. What do you want Les and me to do today?" she asked.

"I'd like for you to go down to the fishing hole and watch for the bear. I need to know if he is still in the area or has gone back up the mountain. If you don't see him today, I'll take an air tour to look for him. The word's out, and Burt Donnigan may not be the only one wanting a big bear hide," advised Ted Wilson.

"Les is in my office waiting to see what our assignment will be today. I'll tell him we're going back to bear country," she was smiling as she left the office.

Minutes later the two officers were on their way back to the ferry landing. They didn't see Gayle, but Betty knew she wasn't far away. They crossed the river and made the walk downstream to their observation spot near the bear's fishing hole. As they watched, they determined sport fishing had slowed somewhat. Fishermen were having to cast many more times before catching a fish. Some of the fishermen were leaving the river early today. It was late in the afternoon when her radio sparked to life. It was Gayle.

"How's it going down there?" she asked.

"Boring as the devil," replied Betty. "I think we'll be leaving in about an hour. We haven't seen any bears today. Have you had any reports of sightings by fishermen?"

"No, I haven't. I don't know if you've noticed, but this run is slowing down and folks are getting restless. I hope they don't start drinking to fill their time on the river." The radio went quiet for a few seconds before Gayle came back on, "Gotta go, there's a fight going on upriver from the ferry."

"Do you need backup?" asked Holden.

"No, I don't think so. If I walk slow, a winner will be crowned before I get there. Bye"

Another hour went by. Finally, not seeing any bears, Holden said to her partner, "What do you think, Les. Should we call it a day and go to town and have dinner at Froso's?"

"I think that's a wonderful idea, Partner," he replied.

They drove back to town and stopped at the classy Greek style restaurant. Froso, the owner/manager was at the reception desk when they entered.

"Hello, Officer Holden! How are you?" she asked.

"Just great, Froso. How's business?" asked Betty.

"It's summertime. It's always busy this time of year, but we always have a booth for you." The very pleasant lady showed them to a booth near the front window, near the back where they could eat without being disturbed.

The dinner was fabulous and the iced tea was sweet. It was a very enjoyable meal of shrimp marsala. It was nice to sit on a soft seat and not a damp log in the woods.

"I'm going to enjoy the evening at home tonight. I'll see you at 0500 tomorrow, Les." She dropped him near his truck and proceeded toward home. It would all begin again tomorrow.

CHAPTER 19

Morning came and Betty had slept well for the first time in many days. She made her way to the kitchen to make coffee and find something for breakfast. She was rinsing her cereal bowl when the phone rang. It was Ted Wilson.

"Sleep well?" he asked.

"I sure did. What's up, Boss?"

"I just wanted to let you know I'm going to be on-air patrol today. Keep your radio handy. I plan to be in your area and look for the bear before noon. If it works out, I'll meet you at the airport and buy you and your partner some lunch at Sunrise Inn."

"You know us, Boss. We'll go anywhere for food." They laughed. "Les and I will be on the riverbank checking licenses and counting stringers."

"Good, I'll see you around noon. I'll buzz the fishing hole when I'm on my way."

Betty finished tidying up the kitchen, strapped on her gun belt and went to her truck. Les was waiting in his vehicle when she arrived. "You're up early this morning," she said as he opened the rear door to put his backpack inside.

"Boy, I slept good last night," he said as he fastened his seatbelt. "What are we doing today?" he asked.

"Same soup, different bowl," she said as she started the truck. "I talked to Sarge this morning and he wants us to check fishermen today. He's going to be flying today and wants to meet us for lunch."

"Are we bear hunting today?" he asked.

"Not this morning. That doesn't mean we won't be out there this afternoon. I guess it depends on what the Sarge finds while he's flying around."

Most of the trip to the ferry landing was spent without conversation. Gayle was sitting in her truck at the landing when they arrived.

"Good morning, Gayle," she greeted as she opened the rear door to retrieve her pack and shotgun.

"Hi, Betty. I bought us some donuts to go with our morning coffee."

The three officers stood near the rear of Gayle's truck, eating pastries and drinking hot, black coffee. Stuffing her thermos back inside her backpack, Betty said, "Well, I guess it's time to go to work."

Gayle stood in the parking lot and watched the ferry cross the river to the other side.

The morning went well, and they checked a large number of licenses. They asked if there had been any bear sightings this morning. One fisherman had seen a small black bear across the river on the highway side. The officers spent the rest of the morning at this chore, while keeping an eye on the wooded area behind the river. It was after eleven o'clock when Holden motioned for them to get back to the ferry crossing. It took several minutes to get to the airport to find Wilson had not yet landed. They would wait.

A half hour later the small blue and white Super Cub landed and taxied to the parking area. Wilson climbed out of the airplane and stretched.

"Sorry I'm a little late, but I spotted a brown bear on the hillside above the river. It took a while to get a good look at him. It wasn't our big old boy. He was a pretty bear, though."

They went to the Sunrise Inn to have lunch and to visit Arden, the owner. As they rode back to the airstrip, the Sergeant asked Les, "Say, young man, how would you like to fly back to town with me?

"Oh, wow, Sarge. Do you mean it?" asked an excited Les Goddard.

"Sure, it'll give you a chance to see what this part of the country is really like." He turned to Betty, "Holden, you can hook up with Gayle and come back later. I'll take Les to the office when we get back."

"I hope he doesn't throw up on you, Sarge" she said jokingly.

She watched the two men strap into the little plane and take off. They flew up Kenai Lake to the other end before returning and flying downriver through the river canyon and over Skilak Lake. Wilson flew up and over the glacier, then back around to the low ridge between Skilak Lake and Tustamena Lake, where they had seen several

small bears, both black and brown. The flyers saw
a small herd of Caribou cooling themselves on a
patch of ice at the base of the glacier. Through the
intercom and headsets Wilson told Les they were
getting low on fuel, and he was heading back to
Soldotna.

Back on the ground, with the airplane tied
down, Ted Wilson asked, "Well, Les, how did you
like flying?"

"Oh, man, I need to learn how to fly. That
was fantastic. Does it cost a lot to learn to fly?"
asked the young officer.

"Yes, I'm afraid it does. But you can enjoy
every minute of it. It takes 40 hours of flying time
to qualify for a license. A couple of our State
pilots are licensed instructors. We can try to get
them to do at least some of your training. But that
would mean you'd have to sign on as a permanent
officer." Wilson was making an offer to the young
man that would change his life and his life's goals.
"Come on. Ride back to the office with me."

The Sergeant invited Goddard to his office
and asked him to sit across from him while he
called someone. It was Roger Dean, a Fish and
Wildlife Protection officer with flight instructor's
credentials. After introducing Goddard and
explaining why he'd called, Wilson handed the
phone to the young officer.

"Hello, Mr. Dean. I'm Les Goddard and
I'm a summer hire. The Sergeant said you might
be able to give me some flight instruction. He also

said it would mean I'd have to become a full-time officer. I think it would be a great opportunity for me. I'm considering the offer. It would mean I'd have to finish most of my college classes via the internet. What do you think, Mr. Dean? Would you be willing to teach me?"

"I'll tell you what I'll do. You meet me at the Soldotna airport and we'll go for a ride. If you can prove to me that you have an aptitude for flying, I'll take you on. That means you will need to apply for a permanent position with the department. It also means you'll need to do a lot of reading about regulations and such. It isn't an easy thing to do, but if you want it bad enough, you'll learn to fly. I can tell you that for me, it's the most enjoyable thing I've ever done. Would you be able to go for a ride this afternoon?"

"Oh, yessir Mr. Dean. What time do you want me to be there?" asked the excited young officer. The arrangements were made, and the enthusiastic young officer thanked the Sergeant for his interest as he left the office to drive to the airport where he would meet Roger Dean.

Three hours later a very tired Betty Holden came into the office and met with Wilson. "How did Les like flying with you, Sarge?" she asked.

The Sergeant chuckled out loud. "He's at the airport right now, taking his first flying lesson. I think he's going to go ahead with it and apply for a full-time position with the department. I really like that young man. He has a good head on his shoulders and like you said, he has a lot of guts and works hard. I think he's going to apply. I'll recommend him to the board."

"That would be great for us. He's proven to be someone I'd like to work alongside."

Wilson scratched his head and asked, "How was the rest of your day?"

"Pretty slow, actually. The sockeye run is slowing down on this first run. They're still catching a lot of fish, but it takes a lot longer to get a limit of salmon these days. I didn't see any bears, but I had a radio call from Gayle while I was driving back to the office. She said there were two young brown bears at the fishing hole. They stayed for about an hour, fishing together. I'm guessing they were brothers the female had kicked out of the house, but they were still running together."

"I'd say your assessment was accurate, Betty. I don't think they'll be any trouble as long as the fishermen don't try to provoke them. You may as well write your report and head home. There's no telling how long Les will be out there flying with Roger."

She went to her office to file the citations she had written today. These would be sent to the DA's office for court hearings. She was finished and relaxing at her desk when Les Goddard came in to see her.

He was beaming, "Did the Sergeant tell you he got me my first ride with a flight instructor?" he asked.

"He sure did. How did it go?" she asked.

"Oh man, I've never done anything that excited me like that. He let me take the controls, steer the plane, and do a couple of things and when we came back, he let me land the plane with his instructions, of course. It was really fun. I've decided I can finish my degree on-line and apply for a position with FWP. Can I use you as a reference?" asked the excited young officer.

Betty held back a chuckle. "Of course, you can," she answered. "Heck, you may be my boss someday."

"I don't know about that, but I think this is a great opportunity for me and I don't want to pass it up."

Les left the office, whistling a tune. Betty watched him leave and remembered how proud she was when she was hired as an officer. It had been a great day in her life, leading to a long and wonderful career.

Goddard was in the parking lot when she arrived the next morning. As he climbed into the seat she asked, "Well, do you have your feet on the ground this morning?"

"Yup, sure do. I'd like to get back to the office a little early today if we can. I have a lot of paperwork to get done here in the office. I'm going to apply for a permanent officer position and there is a lot of paperwork I need to complete."

"I'll see what I can do, Les. I think this is a good decision on your part. Congratulations."

They met Gayle at the ferry landing to have a cup of coffee before crossing the river. "Anything new around here?" asked Holden.

"No, not much," replied Gayle. The crowd of fishermen is beginning to thin out since the run has slowed. But you know how it is, the second run will start in a few days, and it'll all start over again."

"Les and I'll be checking licenses and counting stringers this morning. Les wants to go to the office this afternoon to make an application for a permanent position with the department. He had his first flight with an instructor yesterday and that made him want to become a full-time officer."

Gayle slapped Les on the shoulder, "I think that's a great idea, Les. You'll make a good officer. But remember, you have remember the lessons you learned from the best officer on the force: Old Betty, here."

The officers laughed and finished the coffee, ready to cross on the ferry which was coming their way.

Two hours later, while checking fishermen on the riverbank, there was angry shouting downstream a short distance. The two officers hurried to see what was going on.

On the river's edge two men in chest waders were fighting. A real fistfight which turned into a wrestling match. The two men were rolling around in the shallow river's edge as the officers slid down the steep bank to intervene.

The sight of the uniforms made them stop fighting and step out of the river. Without giving any explanations, both men began to blame the other.

"That guy tried to push me into the river. That's how this started," said one of combatants.

"He crowded me out of my fishing spot while I was releasing a salmon," said the other.

Betty Holden was shaking her head, she took a deep breath and said to them, "OK, children. You play nice or you can go to jail for disturbing the peace. Both of you, show me your licenses," she demanded.

The men complied and she wrote the information in her notebook. "Are you boys going to behave, or am I going to have to take you to jail?"

The larger of the two men shook his head and said, "He can have the fishing hole. It ain't worth fighting over. I'm sorry I caused you any trouble officer. I'm leaving now. I came to have some fun, not to fight."
The other man smiled.

"I don't want to have to come back and arrest you two," said Holden. "This river is big enough for both of you. Just find a different rock to stand on and go back to fishing. If I have to come back, you're both going to take a ride to jail. Got it?" she asked.

One fisherman climbed the bank and walked toward the ferry. The other waded back into the water and resumed fishing. Les and Betty climbed the bank, stood to watch a few minutes to be sure it was over, then continued downstream checking licenses.

When they reached the bear's fishing hole, they turned to walk back to the ferry where they crossed and started the truck. It was time to take Les back to the office.

CHAPTER 20

When Holden and Goddard returned to the office, Holden was ordered to report to the Sergeant's office.

"You wanted to see me?" asked Holden upon entering.

"Yes, I did. Have a seat," he ordered.

She parked in the chair opposite his desk. "What's up, Boss?" she asked again.

"I just had a phone call to say Donnigan and Phelps were released on bail. A few minutes ago, I had another call from Donnigan. He wants to come to the office for a talk. He didn't say what he wanted to talk about. I'd like for you to stick around the office and sit in on the conversation. Are you OK with that?" asked Wilson.

"Sure, but Donnigan may not want me here. I'm the one who arrested him."

"I asked him about that. He said he would like you to be here. Said he knows you'll be fair after he watched what you did for his injured friend, Forsythe. In his words, 'she could have let him die'."

"I guess if you think it's alright, then I'll be here. By the way, how is Forsythe?" she asked.

"The hospital called earlier to tell me Forsythe was awake. He's not strong enough yet for an interview, but he is awake and seems to be getting better. They think the bleeding has stopped and he's getting stronger. He can't eat any food as of now, and is still on IV's, but he's improving. It looks like he'll make it."

"That's good news. I hate it when I lose a patient. Especially after all my carefully planned medical treatment," she said jokingly.

"The whole thing is that he trusts you and wants you here. He said he wanted a chance to thank you for what you did. He also wants to see if he can get his Sako rifle returned. You know the one you found at the attack site."

"I guess that's up to you, Boss. We just found an abandoned rifle in the brush and brought it back for evidence. Since the bear wasn't shot, I guess it's your call. Although it does point a finger at the fact they were hunting and not fishing out there in the woods."

"I talked with the DA about it. He thinks these new charges so soon after the last ones, will encourage the judge to take hunting privileges from all three men for the rest of their lives. I think if that's done, there's no need to keep the rifle. He can sell it even if he can't use it."

"I agree with you, Sarge. When is Donnigan supposed to be here?" she asked.

"He should be here just any time now. He called from his attorney's office in Kenai to say he was on his way. Grab a cup of coffee and I'll page you when he gets here."

Les was at his desk working on forms and applying for a student pilot license when she walked past. She had some citations to work on at her own desk and was still busy with them when Wilson called for her to come to the office for the interview.

Donnigan and Phelps were waiting in the Sergeant's office when she came into the room. They both stood to greet her.

"Officer Holden, I want to thank you for what you did for my friend David. You saved his life, and I can never repay you for what you did."

Burt Donnigan reached out to shake her hand.

"Around here we respect all life, Mr. Donnigan. I was able to give Mr. Forsythe a chance by means of my training. I'm grateful he survived. His injuries were dreadful. I thank you for caring for both me and Mr. Forsythe."

"I know you wouldn't understand my motives. I've been a hunter all my life. I've hunted since I was a young boy. I came to Alaska at a young age, in the Air Force. I came back to Alaska after I left the military to become a big game guide. I've been a guide for a very long time. That part of my life is over now. I regret being such a problem for you, but I became so obsessed with that bear, because he was so beautiful and so large, I just couldn't let him get away. I understand now that was unreasonable. But at the time it was the most important thing in my head. I apologize for what I did." Donnigan was nearly in tears.

"I do understand, Mr. Donnigan, but you must understand that we're here to protect our wildlife and stop any of its abuses. This wasn't a personal thing. We were only doing our job protecting the bear. I'm sorry your friend was injured, but he put himself in this danger. He had a choice, the same as you." Holden was honest with the poacher.

"Yes, and I'm sorry I put him in danger. You have no idea how much I regret this entire incident. It was all my fault. I talked them into it. Nothing could have stopped me from this hunt. I'm sorry." Donnigan was looking at the floor in shame.

"All that being said, Mr. Donnigan," began Sergeant Wilson, "What can we do for you?"

"I came here to apologize for my actions and see if it would be possible to get my Sako rifle back."

"Holden and I have talked about it and agree that if the DA and the judge approve, we'll allow it. Come see us after your court hearing on these charges. I want you to know I thank you for your honesty and forthrightness. I hope this will lead to a different occupation and pleasure in the future. Thank you."

They all shook hands and the visitors left the office.

Holden stopped at Goddard's desk as she passed on her way back to her office. "Hey, Partner, how's it going?"

"I can see a lot of computer time in my future," he said, laughing. "I have to study all the regulations for flying and read about flight principals and all the while work a full shift and keep up on my scholastic studies. It'll be tough, but I hope it'll be worth it. I think it will." He snickered, "Don't tell anyone, but I like this job."

Betty snickered at the joke, "Don't stay here too late. We have to be at work at 0500 tomorrow."

She finished her paperwork and left the office with Les still at his desk. At home she took a long shower and ate a can of soup for dinner. She fell asleep in her chair, waking around midnight. It was time for her to fall into bed. 0400 get up time comes early.

Les was in the parking lot when she arrived. "Did you stay here all night?" she asked when he opened the rear door of the truck.

"No, but I could have. I worked late to finish the application and send a letter to my school asking for an internet curriculum. I guess I've decided," he answered.

Gayle was missing from the ferry crossing parking lot this morning. The officers drank their last cup of coffee for the morning and crossed the river on the ferry. The number of fishermen on the shoreline was dwindling by the day, as the early Sockeye Salmon run dwindled.

"If the bear wasn't our priority, I don't believe we'd be working this area," commented

Betty. "This run is about done and the next one won't start for another two or three weeks. I know it seems like a waste of time, but we have to remember we're here to keep an eye on the big brown bear."

"I was wondering, will the bear leave this area when this run dies out?" he asked.

"Sometimes they leave and sometimes they just go into the woods and catch any little animals they can catch. The sad thing is they kill a lot of calf moose during this time. These bears are the cause of the demise of most of the calves that die this time of year." Holden was speaking from data published by Fish and Game biologists.

"If we don't see any sign of the big bear today, I'll ask Sarge for a couple of days off for both of us." She looked at him and smiled, then said, "Heck, you might get some time go flying."

In the late afternoon Holden decided it would be worth going into the woods to look for fresh bear sign. The search was fruitless. It looked as if the bears had left the area several days prior. With this finding they began the trek back to the ferry crossing to return to the office.

At the office she spoke with the Sergeant, "I know you're short of officers, Sarge, but Les and I haven't had much time off and have been working some long hours. Do you think we could take a couple of days off?"

Wilson scratched his head and replaced his cap, "I guess you're right, Holden. If you're convinced the bears have left the area, go ahead. Take three days off but be available in case I need you to go to court for something. I'll go to court for the Donnigan case. I can take care of that for now."

"Thanks, Sarge. You might call Roger Dean and have him take Les out flying if he has time. The kid is really pumped up about learning to fly."

"I'll talk with Goddard and see if he's up to it. If so, I'll get in contact with Dean. Go on now and get out of here before I change my mind."

Roger Dean called Les Goddard, asking him to meet him at the airport. It was time for another session of instruction. This time Les would be in the front seat of the small Piper Super Cub while Roger sat in the rear giving instructions. Les had landed the aircraft from the rear seat in the last session, but this time he would be doing many other maneuvers. The session lasted nearly two hours and upon landing Les was given further instruction in regulations regarding airport protocols. He told the young Goddard he would need to go to a doctor to get a flight physical.

By the end of this session Les was completely convinced he had made the right decision about applying for a permanent position. The hours of flight time were better than a larger paycheck. He arranged to use his days off to go on air patrol with Roger to learn what they do and what they look for. He'd also learn the capabilities of the small airplane. Landing on open tundra or very short clearings were hair-raising at first, but he learned to like the adventures.

Early the second morning of his three days off, he went to the doctor for his flight physical. He was able to get in quickly because he was a State employee and this affected his employment.

Meanwhile, at the Russian River Ferry, Gayle had finished checking licenses and looking for the big brown bear. There had been several brown bears at the fishing hole, but none were the big brute they were watching.

The riverbanks were not as crowded these days, as the early run of salmon had finished. The second run had not yet begun. The fish had entered the lower river, but it would take several days for them to begin to enter the Russian River. These fish were usually larger and heavier than those of the early run. These were the fish that drew the large crowds of fishermen from all over the world. They came from Germany, Switzerland and many other countries around the globe.

Many years ago, the military allowed training flights from bases in California and other States to bring loads of fishermen to Alaska, putting them in buses and bringing them to this river to fish. Others would be allowed to take small cargo type aircraft to small airstrips and lodges on the Alaska Peninsula to fish those rivers for Sockeye, Silver Salmon and King Salmon, all far away from the city crowds of the Kenai Peninsula.

The afternoon of his flight physical, Les was scheduled to fly with Roger. Roger called to tell him he could go with him but couldn't sit in the front seat this time. They were going to Lake Illiamna to search for a missing fisherman somewhere on the South shore of the huge lake.

It took more than two hours to fly to the airport at Illiamna where they refueled the small airplane and took off again for the other side of the lake. The sector assigned to them was on the upper end of the huge lake and required them to fly a search area of more than two hundred square miles. The weather was good, the scenery was beautiful and Les sat in the back seat of the airplane with a pair of binoculars, scanning the shoreline for any signs of the missing fisherman or his boat.

They'd searched for more than two hours when Les spotted something he thought could be a capsized boat. Dropping low over the object, Dean agreed this could be the missing fisherman's boat. He radioed search headquarters to advise them and asked for a boat to come check the capsized craft. Roger flew a wide circle in an attempt to locate the fisherman, but there was only open water for miles in every direction. On his last circle before returning for fuel, they flew over the shoreline for several miles when Les saw a man on the beach, waving his arms.

Roger dropped low to view the rocky beach and decided he could land there. He sent a radio message to Illiamna search headquarters asking that a search vessel come to the site. He gave them the GPS coordinates.

Roger landed the aircraft on the short, rocky, landing site where the fisherman was waiting. He ran toward the airplane and Roger shut down the engine. He opened the door on the left side of the aircraft as the man approached. Roger was first out of the plane with Les close behind.

"Oh, thank God, thank God." The man shouted as he ran toward the pilot. "I didn't think anyone would ever find me. I've been here three days and I haven't seen anyone. Thank God you came."

Roger held up his hands, "Hold on there, fella. Are you OK? Are you injured?" he asked.

"No, I'm good. I am just so happy to see you. Thank God."

"OK then. I have a boat coming to pick you up. We'll wait with you until they get here."

"Oh, thank you. Thank God." He said over and over.

"I don't have any food in the airplane, but I'm sure the folks on the boat will have something for you to eat."

An hour later the boat was spotted heading in their direction. When it arrived and the man was loaded aboard. Roger and Les climbed back into the Cub and started the engine. They refueled the airplane again in Illiamna before returning to Soldotna.

CHAPTER 21

It was late when they landed back at Soldotna. Les helped Roger fuel the airplane and tie it down for the night.

"I'll take care of the report tonight, Les. Thanks for the help. You did a great job today. Sorry you didn't get a chance to fly, but this was business and it had to end with everyone surviving, even us." They both laughed at the joke. "Be sure you put the hours down on your time sheet. You earned it today."

Les Goddard knew after this long day, he'd made the right decision in applying for a permanent position. Learning to fly will be a definite bonus, he thought. He was hungry and stopped to get a burger on his way from the airport. There was no hurry in getting home, as he didn't think he would be able to sleep thinking about his exciting day. He felt joy and pride in a job well done, knowing the man they had been looking for was found alive and in good condition.

Exhaustion soon overtook his excitement and he slept like a log. In the morning, he felt a need to tell someone about his day flying with Roger. The only one he could think of sharing this with was Betty Holden. He called her to ask if it was alright for him to come to her house and tell her about it all. She said it was.

He stopped at the local Safeway store to buy some pastries on his way to her place. She was waiting for him and let him into the house. She saw pride in his stature as he entered with the donuts.

"I take it you had a good time yesterday." She said with a smile.

Les was beaming with pride, "I can't tell you how good it was to be on that search. The flying and seeing some of the State I'd never seen before was great. But to be a part of a rescue, knowing we saved a man's life…well I can't tell you how good it made me feel. I just had to share that with someone, and it turned out to be you. You've been so good to me and taught me so much. I'm truly grateful for that."

"Don't sell yourself short, Les. You did all the right things. All I did was let you know some things about the job. You applied those things to each situation pretty well. I hope you take that permanent position they offered you."

"I've already filled out the application. I have a flight physical scheduled for next week. I've contacted my college and asked to be put on an online curriculum. I just can't tell you how much I enjoy this work. Thanks for letting me be your partner."

Holden smiled and said, "I hope you always feel this good about the job. It can be frustrating sometimes, but that's true with almost any job, anywhere. You're going to make a good officer, Les. Don't ever lose that enthusiasm."

"We have one more day off and I have laundry and housecleaning to get done. I guess I'd better go home and start getting caught up. Thanks for listening to me, Partner." He stood to leave, then turned to make one more comment, "If I ever get as good at this job as you, I'll owe you even more. Thanks again, Betty."

Holden watched as Les drove from her driveway. "Come to think about it," she thought, "I guess I'd better get some housework done, too."

Monday morning came and at 0500 she drove into the parking lot where Les was waiting in his vehicle. She waited while he loaded his gear into the rear seat of her truck and climbed into the passenger seat.

"Well, Partner, did you get rested up?" she asked.

He chuckled a little, "It was tough shutting my excitement down and get to sleep the other night, but I finally did."

"I had a note on my desk wanting me to bring you back early today. Roger Dean said he was giving you a check-ride and arranging for you to begin solo flights. He'll give you all the dos and don'ts. He's a good officer and you should listen to him."

"Is that going to interfere with our bear patrol duty?" he asked.

"I don't think it will. No one has seen the bear in several days. He may have moved on to find another food source, like a moose calf or something. We'll see what Gayle has to say when we get there."

Gayle was waiting for them at the ferry landing and waved as they parked.

"Hi, Gayle, did you miss us?" said Betty with a smile.

"Sure did. I had to drink all that coffee and eat all the donuts by myself."

"Two things, Gayle. First, how's the fishing?" asked Holden.

"Last night there were some big reds caught near the ferry. It looks like the second run may be starting. If it is, you can count on a lot of fishermen. What's the other thing," asked Gayle.

"The other thing is, has anyone reported seeing the big brown bear?"

"There have been a few brownies fishing in several places downstream from here, but the big one hasn't been reported to me," Gayle responded in a more serious tone.

"Well, I guess we get busy checking licenses and counting fish," said Holden. "Les needs to get back to town early today. He's having a check-ride that will allow him to fly solo in the State plane. He was an observer on a search at Lake Illiamna this week. I think he liked it."

"Well, congratulations, Les," replied Gayle.

"Thanks, Gayle, I've applied for a permanent position with FWP. The Sarge said he would recommend me. I hope it all works out in my favor."

"Good luck today, guys" said Gayle as she climbed into her truck.

The huge crowd of fishermen hadn't yet reached the river to attack the second run of Sockeye Salmon and there was only a smattering of fishermen on the riverbanks. The officers checked fishermen as they went downstream. As they approached the bear's fishing hole, Betty said, "Let's go up into the woods and look for any sign of the big bear. Keep your shotgun handy, though. He's not the only bear in the woods and we could meet up with one of his cousins."

Les agreed and checked to be sure there was a cartridge in the chamber.

They searched the woods for almost an hour and came across a trail leading up the hillside. There were many bear tracks in the loose dirt of the trail. Betty motioned for Les to follow her up the trail. They hiked up the hillside until they ran out of the spruce timber and only willows and alders covered the hillside. The bear trail continued up the hill through the brush for another several hundred yards.

They had climbed high above the tree line and were about to leave the willows, to an expanse of grassy slopes. Standing at the edge of the brushy cover they surveyed the hillsides. The trails seemed to disperse into many directions at this point. With binoculars they studied the entire area. They saw no movement anywhere. Above the grassy hillside were rocky, barren slopes leading to the glacier. They finally spotted a mountain goat on a rocky outcrop over the ice of the glacier. Betty pointed it out to Les and they watched it for several minutes.

"I don't see any bears, Les. I think, at least for now, the big bear has gone up into the hills below the glacier. He may be looking for a moose or caribou calf to eat. He's a big bear and he requires more than a rabbit or parka squirrel to satisfy his appetite. I think we should ask the Sarge to fly around and look for him. In the meantime, I think our bear watching days may be over, at least for now."

"You know, I'm supposed to be taking a check-ride this afternoon and I may be able to get Roger to let me fly up around this area to take a look around. What do you think?" he asked.

"If you're going to be out here flying anyway, it might pay off. Just remember, you're supposed to be flying the airplane and not watching for bears. Let Roger do the looking. I don't want to lose a partner at this point."

Les laughed, "I guess that's good advice, Partner. I'll try to remember it."

"For now, I think we should head back down and go up to the ferry landing to head back home. It's going to be a long walk back from here," she said, taking one last look around the hillside.

It took nearly two hours to get back to the ferry crossing. It was an easy walk, most of it downhill. It was another hour before they reached the office, where Roger was waiting for Les.

"Hi Betty," he greeted as she stepped out of her truck. "I see you brought my student back to the office."

"I had to. He can't keep his mind on fish when all he can talk about is flying." The officers laughed at Les' expense.

"Officer Dean," Goddard asked, "Holden and I have been up near the Russian River looking for a big brown bear and followed a trail up the mountainside but couldn't see any sign of him. Do you think we could fly up and around the area to take a short look for it?"

"It depends on you, you're the pilot. I'm only going along for the ride to see if you're qualified to do it alone. If you do go there, I'll do the looking and you do the flying," Roger instructed his student.

With Roger in the back seat, Les made a normal take-off and climb-out. Roger had told him he could fly in any direction he liked as long as it was allowed, and he felt comfortable flying there.

Les had chosen to fly up the river to a short distance below the bear's fishing hole. Then he turned and climbed as the terrain rose and crisscrossed the area looking for bears. On the upper reaches of the hillside and below the glacier they spotted a large blond color brown bear. It looked like a young female, grazing on grasses on the hillside. Les did a good job flying and keeping the distance from the mountain and his wingtips quite large and safe. Roger was impressed with the judgement shown by his young pilot.

"OK Les," Roger said through the headsets. "Let's head back to the airport. You can choose the route."

He chose to fly over the low hillsides, turning toward the airport a few miles south of Soldotna. He called to let traffic at the uncontrolled airport know he was landing and on which runway.

Once on the ground he taxied to the State parking area and shut down the engine. He climbed out of the small cockpit and held the door open to allow Roger to climb out of the rear seat.

He ordered Les to go directly to the tiedown without refueling. As they tied the aircraft down, Roger told his student he would sign off on the student license to verify Les was qualified to fly solo.

It was a proud moment for the young man.

Roger slapped him on the shoulder and congratulated him on a job well done. "I was impressed with the good judgement and care you displayed today. If you always fly like that you'll never get into trouble."

"I want to confess I learned a lot about those judgements when I flew that search with you the other day. You were busy flying and probably didn't think about it, but I watched how you kept up your airspeed and only watched where you were going and not at the ground. It was impressive. I felt safe with your flying skills. I only hope I can be half as good a pilot as you." Les was being honest, and he was truly grateful.

Betty Holden had gone home from the office by the time he returned, but he went inside to call her and report that he was back on the ground.

"Did he sign you off to fly alone?" asked Holden.

"Yes, he did. He said I could fly the State plane if no one had it scheduled for some other duty. I can't believe how lucky I am to be able to do all this flying without it costing me an arm and a leg. I guess I have you to thank for all that."

"Don't thank me. Thank Sergeant Ted Wilson. He likes you and asked Roger to set all this up for you. Ted wants you to stay with Fish and Wildlife Protection. I kinda like the idea myself. Don't be late in the morning." She almost hung up the phone, then remembered another question. "By the way, Les, did you go up to look for the bear?"

"Yes, we did. We only saw one big blond bear. It looked like a female according to Roger, but we didn't see any others."

"Well, good job, Les. See you in the morning."

CHAPTER 22

The next morning they resumed a normal daily schedule, meeting at the office at 0500. Les was several minutes late. He began to apologize the moment he opened the rear door of the truck.

"Sorry I'm late, Holden," he said as he opened the front door to get into the passenger seat. "I had trouble getting to sleep last night and overslept this morning."

"I understand, but don't make it a habit. We have a duty and responsibility to the people of Alaska, and that duty should be taken seriously." She looked at his sad face, "Want some coffee to travel on?" she asked.

"I have some in my pack. I can get it while we're travelling up the road." He reached into his pack in the rear seat and brought out his thermos. "Want some?" he offered.

"Thanks, but I'll wait until we get to the ferry landing."

"You know," he said between sips of hot coffee, "I learned a lot about the lay of the land after seeing it from the air. We took a heck of a hike the other day when we walked up above tree line."

"Yeah, but I liked it. It was fun for me, getting out of the office and hiking in the woods." She paused, "Say, you flew around up there, did you see any place that bear would have gone?"

"No. I asked Roger about that, too. He said the bear could be down below in the trees where we wouldn't see him. He also said he may have gone up the mountain to the glacier to find a baby caribou. We were running out of time, so we didn't fly up to the glacier. That would have been fun, though. We did see some caribou up the mountain on the glacier ice as we flew back to the airport."

Holden chuckled, "I've seen them up there. They like to lay on the ice and keep cool, being where the mosquitoes don't bother them. I was told once that, out on the Alaska Peninsula, the caribou and moose lose more than a pint of blood a day from mosquitoes sucking on them. That seemed like a lot to me, but I've seen the rumps of those animals completely covered with those little biters. By fall their rumps will be one huge scab from bug bites."

"That's amazing," he said. "How do people survive out there?"

"You'll learn they have State regulations about that. If you go out there in the summer, you're required to have a head net for each passenger. Once you experience it you won't ever forget to take the head nets along."

Gayle was waiting in the parking lot again this morning. "Good morning to ya'," she greeted as they stepped out of the truck. "I have a thermos of hot coffee and some Maple bars," she held up a small white paper bag.

"Sounds good to me. Thanks Gayle. Have you had any reports of the bear?" asked Holden.

"I've asked a lot of people the past couple of days, and no one has seen it. Some smaller bears have been seen on the river all the way up to here at the ferry landing." Gayle served Maple bars and coffee.

Conversation silenced while they ate the pastries.

"Well, it looks like we'll have to go to work," said Holden as the ferry started its return trip to this side of the river. "Thanks for the goodies."

The day went slowly because of the increasing number of fishermen working this second run of Sockeye Salmon. The officers had just climbed up the steep bank when Les saw movement near the tree line.

"I think there's a bear coming right now," he said, pointing at the woods.

"Oh, I see him. He's the wrong color for our bear, though. Keep an eye on him and we'll warn the fishermen when we see where he's headed."

A minute later he'd picked a trail to the river a short way downstream. Betty stepped to the edge of the high bank and called to the fishermen below to warn them of the approaching bear. She gave them an indication as to where she thought the bear would come down the bank. The fishermen parted, moving both upstream and downstream, allowing a wide area for the bear to use.

"I guess we'd better stick around a while to watch this bear do its fishing. We don't want him chewing up a tourist."

Les laughed at her remarks.

The bear stood on the high bank for a long while, looking at the river and the fishermen. He finally made his way down the embankment and waded into the water. He caught his first salmon on his third try and carried it to the shore to eat it, then waded into the water again to repeat the process, paying no further attention to the fishermen.

After almost an hour of fishing, the bear climbed the high bank, shook the water from his fur, took one last look at the river and wandered off toward the woods a city block away.

"I really hate to leave here with a bear in the area, but it's getting late. We may as well head back to the office." She paused a few seconds, then added, "Can you think of anything else to do today?"

"No, but when we get back, I'm going to ask if I can use the airplane to get some flying hours. If I can, I'm going to fly up here and search the upper reaches on the mountain to see if I can spot our bear."

"I don't know if that's such a good idea, Les. Do you feel comfortable flying and looking without a spotter?" she asked.

He chuckled, "Don't worry, Betty, I'm not going to fly close to the ground and I'm not going to take any chances. I appreciate your concerns, though."

"I'd hate to see you crash the State plane, that's all," she said.

"You have a right to be concerned, but I know enough about the terrain and my skills to leave a lot of room for error. Thanks for the warning, though." Both officers were mostly silent on the trip back to the office. Holden was writing her daily report when Les entered her office.

"I just talked with Roger. He said I could take the Cub for a ride," he said.

"I guess he thinks you're capable of going out there alone but be careful. I don't want to have to break in a new partner," she cautioned.

Les was laughing as he left the office to go to the airport.

Betty was at home, just finishing her dinner when her phone rang. It was Les and he seemed excited.

"Hey, Holden, it's me. I just got back, and I found the bear. He's high up in a small canyon near the top of the mountain. He's killed a cow moose and is having dinner as we speak. I think that adult moose will keep him fed for a few days."

"I'm glad you're back in one piece, Les. Exactly where did you see the bear?" she asked.

"You know that ridge all the bear trails lead into? It's up that ridge. Nearly to the top and on the left side in a small canyon. There's no real brush, just a grassy sidehill. It looked like a fresh kill, and he hasn't begun to hide it yet," he reported.

Holden thought for a few seconds, then said, "It sounds like we can report to work a little late tomorrow. All we'll be doing, unless there's some emergency, is check licenses and counting stringers. I'll call Gayle and let her know we're going to be late tomorrow. Good job, Les. You know, of course, you can't claim overtime for finding the bear. You're already well-paid by the State for your flight time," she was laughing out loud. "See you at 0700."

Holden arrived at the office an hour earlier to speak with the Sergeant. He was in his office when she arrived. "Hi, Sarge," she greeted.

"You're a little behind schedule, aren't you Holden?" he commented.

"That's why I came to your office. Les went flying last night and found the bear high up on the mountain. Les said the bear had killed a cow moose and was feeding on it when he saw her. It's in a small canyon on the left side of the main ridge above the bear's fishing hole. I told him to come in at 0700 since the bear wouldn't be likely to come to the fishing hole this morning. I thought that since the bear we've been watching wasn't likely to come down while he had a fresh meal on his plate, we'd come in a little late this morning. I hope that was OK with you, Boss."

"Actually, that was really good thinking, and I want you two to go back to the same area and check licenses and creel counts, but I still want you to watch for any bears coming to the river. We don't want any of our bears eating a tourist," Wilson said in a pleasant tone.

The two FWP officers were at the Russian River ferry crossing before eight o'clock. Gayle was waiting when they arrived.

"You guys sure have a cushy job," she said as they climbed from the truck. "I suppose you'll be wanting to go home early, too!" she was laughing as she teased them. She was holding a very large thermos and offering coffee as she laughed.

"Sunup to sundown, nothing more," quipped Betty as she held out her coffee cup.

"It's a good thing the days are getting shorter or you two would be late getting here and leaving." Again, she laughed at the pair as she poured coffee.

Betty sipped her cup of strong, black coffee while Gayle poured for Les. "OK, Gayle, you've had your fun. Tell me, has there been any excitement while we were away last night?" she asked.

"No, nothing very exciting. I'm beginning to see a lot of over-limits. The fangs are growing on the Red Salmon fishermen. You know how it works. I had one at the campground who came back to his camper with a limit and changed clothes and returned to the river to catch some more fish. His wife was canning fish in the camper while he was on the riverbank. We used to see a lot of that in the old days, but not so much these days. I also had several fishermen stashing fish in the ferns along the river and taking them back to the campers in their backpacks. Several tickets I've written were for snagging fish. Some of these fishermen think the mouth goes clear to the tail." Gayle was listing some of the violations she had seen recently.

"What about fights for fishing spots?" asked Betty.

"Not much, but the big crowds are just now arriving. They're sure to get territorial soon." Both officers laughed. Les barely understood what they were saying.

Betty finished her coffee and turned to her partner, "Well, I guess it's about time for us to go to work Pard."

They crossed on the ferry, which was completely full, and began the walk downstream. Gayle had been correct, there were lots more fishermen on the shore, standing only a few inches apart. This was bound to cause trouble before long, thought Holden.

The officers worked their way down-stream, checking licenses as they went. There were a lot of questions asked by non-residents as they went on their way. Betty patiently answered them all.

The officers were only a quarter the way to the bear's fishing hole when they witnessed the first fight of the day. Luckily the men had stepped out of the water before fisticuffs began. Les ran down the steep high bank with Betty following. Goddard stepped between the fighting men and ordered them to stop. They were in their low 30's age-wise, both were strong and healthy. One combatant attempted to push Les aside but was met with a strong push back.

Betty stepped up beside the man behind Les and motioned for him to step back. He complied.

The man facing Les began a step forward, but when he saw the look on the officer's face he backed down.

"Good choice," said Les. "Show me your license," he demanded.

The fisherman complied, reluctantly.

"I could cite you for any number of violations Mister, but I'm in a good mood. Now tell me, what's this altercation about?"

The man gave a huge sigh, "Every time I cast out, this dummy casts his line over me and we tangle up. I don't need that. After about an hour of it I couldn't take it any longer and shoved him toward shore." The fisherman was being honest.

Les turned to the other man, "Is what he said true?" he asked.

"Mostly, but I didn't do it on purpose. He was fishing too close to me, and I couldn't help it if I got tangled with him."

"Where are you from, Sir?" asked Les.

"I'm from Kansas," he replied.

Les turned to the other fighter, "Where are you from,"

"Fairbanks," he said.

Goddard shook his head, "You should be kinder and more tolerant of the visitors to our State. I know the riverbank is crowded, but if you live in Alaska, you know visitors aren't well versed on riverbank protocols. Be kind to them. Now, I don't care if you both fish in the same area, but I would suggest one of you find another spot. Since you're a resident, I'd suggest you be the one to find another fishing spot." Les remained between the men.

"Oh, Hell. I'll find another spot," the man agreed.

Goddard spoke to the men, "I want you both to know if I have to come back again, I'll write the both of you tickets and have you both taken to jail for being a public nuisance."

The man he'd been facing took a few steps to pick up his backpack and began to climb the steep bank.

Holden turned to the man she'd been standing near, "I think you have a little more room to fish now. My partner is correct. If we have to come back, we won't be so patient."

The tourist seemed happy over not being cited, "Yes, Ma'am," he said as he waded back into the water.

The rest of the day was less challenging and more repetitive.

CHAPTER 23

When the day ended the officers were returning to the office and Holden turned to Goddard, "That was a great job you did out there today, Les. I was impressed with the tact you displayed, and I was really impressed when you showed the fisherman from Fairbanks you could back it up. You did a great job. I'm happy you decided to take a permanent position with Fish and Wildlife."

"I've never liked bullies," said Les, but I don't think this guy was a bully. He just got tired of being crowded from his fishing spot. I didn't think it looked like fishing was much fun there either. I've never seen a fishing spot with five thousand fishermen all trying to fish the same fishing hole. It's crazy."

"It's this way every year, Les. This is the most famous fishing hole in the world. People come here from every corner of the earth to fish and have a good time. You've seen and talked with folks who hardly speak or understand English. Most fishermen are cooperative, but sometimes their patience wears thin. It's our job to keep the peace and enforce the fishing regs. You did a wonderful job of that today."

Back at the FWP office Betty told Les he should come into the office with her to help with an explanation to the Sergeant.

At his office door she found him deep in concentration over a document on his desk.

"Hi, Sarge," she said before entering. "Can we come in for a couple of minutes?"

He looked up from his desk. "Oh, sure, Holden. Come on in," he said, closing the folder on his desk.

The officers entered and sat across from him.

"You're early today," he commented. "What's up?"

"Nothing, really. We had a confrontation today that we thought we should report to you in person."

He sat up straight in his chair.

"It wasn't anything too bad, Boss. Les here, had to get a little physical with a fisherman up at Russian River. We'd been checking licenses all the way down the river from the ferry crossing when there was an argument and a fight breaking out between fishermen on the river. Les here, jumped off the high bank and got between the two. I followed him down and faced off with the less aggressive of the men. Les backed the other one off and gave him one of the best lectures I've ever heard. He told them he wasn't going to cite them, but if they went back to fighting, he was going to arrest them and have them taken to jail. That seemed to stop the fisticuffs. He did an excellent job of convincing one fighter to leave the area and teaching the other about courtesy at the fishing grounds. I considered this one of the best solutions I had ever seen."

Wilson closed his eyes and shuddered before saying anything. "OK Officers, do I need to start to take notes on this incident?"

"I don't think so, Sarge. I only wanted to let you know how great this young man defused the situation, resolved the problem and prevented a recurrence of the problem. When we stepped over the high bank and ran to the river's edge, I thought we were going to be in a fight. But this guy took care of it without letting the situation get to that point," explained Holden.

"OK," said the Sergeant with another big sigh. "Les, I want you to write me a full report giving me your version of what took place." He turned to Holden, "Holden, I want you to write me a full report of the incident from your viewpoint. It sounds to me as if you both did a wonderful job of stopping a fight. But if either one of those men comes in here to file a complaint, I want to be able to give them your assessment of what happened. Now go to your offices and get busy." As they stood to leave he added, "By the way. Good job, guys."

Two hours later they left the office. Their statements had been entered into the computer for Wilson to read in the morning.

They walked to the parking lot together where Holden said. "Have a good evening, Les. Let's try 0700 again tomorrow morning."

"Thanks for backing me up again Holden. You're a pretty good instructor." He was smiling as he walked to his truck.

Holden watched him drive away and reached for her radio to call Gayle and tell her about the new arrival time.

The next morning, Gayle was waiting at the ferry landing when they arrived, holding that giant thermos bottle high for them to see as they drove into the parking area.

"I don't know how you two get these bankers hours," she said as they stepped out of the truck.

"Just lucky I guess," said Holden as she held out her coffee cup for filling. "Anything new this morning?" she asked.

"Yes, there was another bear incident last night in the campground. This time it was a black bear. No one was injured this time, thank God. But this bear completely tore up a visitor's camp. We found out later this visitor had an entire cooler of smoked salmon in his tent. The bear completely wrecked the camp and ate most of the fish in the cooler. The owner of the tent had been down at the campfire area drinking beer with friends when it took place. He came back in time to see the bear leaving the mess."

"I'm glad he didn't attack the camper. Black bears usually kill and eat the ones they attack. I guess he was full of smoked salmon and wasn't hungry," said Holden.

The three officers laughed. "What's on your schedule today, Betty?" asked Gayle.

"We'll be checking licenses from here to the canyon, just like we've been doing the past few days. Is there anything we should be looking for?"

"Nope, nothing special. I'm still a little worried about that giant bear that had been here. No one has seen him for about a week and the run is going to peak soon. I think he's going to want some more fish before the end of the run." Gayle had a concerned look on her face as she spoke.

"Ah, don't worry, Gayle. If the bear comes back, we can have old Les here talk to him and convince him to leave." All three officers laughed again and Les nearly choked on his coffee.

By late afternoon the two officers had worked their way to a spot downstream from Jim's Landing and above the rapids of the canyon. There were several fishermen in the area, and all seemed to be doing well. The second fisherman they checked had at least two times the legal limit on his stringer. His partner, fishing a few yards down river, had even more fish. The two men were cited for being over limit and their licenses were taken by the FWP officers. The weight of the fish seized was so great they loaded their own backpacks with fish, as well as the backpacks of the fishermen. The officers had the men carry their backpacks upriver to the ferry crossing where the officers took possession of the backpacks and fishing rods. They gave the fishermen a court date and allowed them to leave.

Holden and Goddard loaded the backpacks and fish into their truck and began the drive back to the office. It had been a very long and strenuous day for them both.

"I'm going to enjoy my shower tonight," claimed Goddard.

"Me too, Partner," said Holden, "That's the largest overlimit I've seen in recent years. I'm glad we were able to get the men to carry those packs back to the truck."

Holden called Gayle on the radio to say they were leaving for the day. She drove back toward the office when there was a radio call from an officer on Mystery Creek Road, asking for assistance.

Holden used the radio in the truck to answer the call. "C-23, this is C-11. What do you need?"

"Oh, good, C-11. I have a man here with severe injuries, a broken leg and very bad bleeding lacerations. I'm ten miles up Mystery Creek Road and I need help getting this man out of here. Can you help me get him to my truck? I've called an ambulance, but it's going to take a long time for them to get here. I want to drive him down to the parking area near the Sterling Highway."

"We're almost to the Mystery Creek Road, but it'll take several minutes to drive the ten miles to your location. I'm on my way to you now."

"Good, I'll try to stop the bleeding. Try to get here quickly. C-23 out"

Betty turned to Les, "It looks like it'll be a while getting these fish in the cooler, but this injured person is more important right now."

"I certainly agree with you on that one," said Les.

They turned onto the gravel road, but kept a high rate of speed, causing a large cloud of dust to rise behind the State pickup. Fifteen minutes after the initial radio call they arrived at the FWP truck parked at the side of the road. Holden picked up the mic and called C-23, "Where are you?" she asked.

"The trail on the north side of the road. Not quite a mile up here. I can't leave this guy. Without a stretcher we'll have to carry him back to the truck. Get here as quickly as possible. He's lost a lot of blood and I need some help."

"We're on our way. Ten minutes." She motioned for Les to follow as she began to jog up the trail. Minutes later they rounded a curve in the trail and saw the other officer on the trail, kneeling alongside someone. As they approached, they could see the officer was holding a compress on an abdominal wound of some sort.

"Les, dig out the medical kit from your backpack," ordered Holden as they approached.

There was a lot of blood under the victim, and it was plain to see he had a compound fracture of his right lower leg. The bone was protruding through his pantleg.

Don Lewis, "C-23", was tending the injured hiker.

"Did he say how it happened, Don?" asked Betty.

"He's passed out now, probably from loss of blood, but he was able to talk when I arrived. He said he had been attacked by an irate moose he'd met on the trail. I don't know how we're going to get him back to the road, but we have to stop this bleeding before we can move him." Lewis said.

Betty bent to help Lewis with the wound. Les stood by, thinking. Finally, he said, "You two take care of his bleeding problem and I'm going to make a sling to load him on my back to carry him out."

It took a half hour for the officers to stop the abdominal bleeding. They invented a splint to keep his leg bones from doing any more damage as they carried him out of the woods.

When he'd been stabilized, Betty asked Lewis, "How the heck did you even find this guy?"

"He'd taped a note to his driver's side mirror. Someone he knew must have been coming to follow him up the trail, so I followed to see what he was up to and came across him here. He said he was just walking up the trail when a cow moose came out of the brush and attacked him. She stomped him, knocked him down and stomped him some more. I haven't seen the moose, but I'll bet she has a calf in the brush near here. I haven't had a chance to look for tracks."

Just then, Les Goddard returned. He'd been to the truck to get a few things to fabricate a seat and a strap to hold the injured man him in it, all attached to straps of one of the backpacks.

"Here we go, guys," said Les, holding up the contraption. "I'm going to put this on my shoulders and I want you two to load him onto the seat and strap him to it really tight."

Holden shrugged her shoulders, "That's a lot of weight for you to carry, Les," she said with doubt in her voice.

"It's less than a mile to the truck and the trail is mostly downhill. I should only need to carry him for about ten minutes. When we get there, it'll be up to you two to lay him down in the back of the truck. I threw some padding in the bed of our truck to lay him on. Now, I think we'd better get him down there before he tries to wake up."

"Ok, Les, let's get at it."

Les slipped into the harness and squatted alongside the injured man. Lewis and Holden wrestled the limp body into position and strapped him to the backpack. They helped Les return to his feet with the weight on his back. The makeshift seat seemed to work. Lewis checked to make sure the straps were tight and said, "OK Les, we'll walk alongside him, but the trail is narrow and only one of us will be able to hold him in place. We'll let you know if we need to adjust the load. Now, let's get going."

They managed to keep the unconscious man in place and he remained unaware of his ride. It took several minutes to arrive at the truck on the side of the road. The tailgate had been left down and Les rested the weight there while Betty and Don took off the straps and laid the limp body on the blankets Les had placed there.

"The medical kit is there," he said, pointing to the front of the pickup bed. "You two get in with him and I'll drive us back to the highway. The ambulance should be there by now."

They wasted no time climbing into the truck while Les slipped into the driver's seat. He drove carefully to avoid jarring the injured man too badly. They saw the flashing lights of the ambulance as they neared the highway and Les tweaked his siren an instant to let them know they were near.

The medics were amazed when they saw what the three FWP officers had done to care for this patient. They did their best to stabilize him and loaded him into the ambulance for transport. The officers watched the red lights and heard the siren as they drove away, toward town.

Holden was smiling, "Well, let's go get your truck and go to the office to write reports."

"I sure do thank you two," said Lewis. "I'm glad you were in the neighborhood. If it weren't for you two, I don't think he'd have made it." He turned to Les, "Young man, that was a great piece of 'bush engineering' you did."

"Let's go to town, guys," said Betty.

CHAPTER 24

It had been very late the previous evening when Holden had finished her daily reports and gone home. She told Les to do an abbreviated report and go home early. In the office she called the hospital to check on the injured man they treated the night before. The hospital told her he had been sent back to surgery this morning and there was nothing to report on his condition.

While she had been on the telephone with the hospital, Ted Wilson entered the office to begin his daily routine. She decided to go to his office and give him a first-hand report of the incident.

"Hi, Sarge. Got a minute?" she asked.

"Sure. Have a seat. I want to hear about the injured hiker you treated last night. You and your partner seem to create a lot of action everywhere you go," he said with a smile.

"You should have been there, Sarge. Lewis and I worked on the hiker to stop his bleeding and Goddard went back to the truck to create a backpack that worked like a wheelchair. It was something to see. He brought it back to where we were, we loaded the unconscious man on Les' back. Lewis and I walked behind to watch the hiker. Les kept a steady pace all the way to the truck. He 'd already made a sort of bed for the patient. Lewis and I sat in back with him, Les drove the truck to the highway where the ambulance was waiting." She was shaking her head and smiling, "I've never seen anything like it."

"I had a call from the hospital last night to tell me they were going to sedate him to allow them to pump some more blood into him before they took him back to surgery to complete the job of repairing his ripped-up abdomen. They also told me the three of you probably saved this man's life." The Sergeant took off his cap to scratch his scalp.

"Sarge, this young man is phenomenal. This is the second time in two days he's demonstrated extraordinary skills. He's going to make an exceptional officer," she smiled and said, "But, if you tell him I said that I'll deny it."

They laughed. Holden returned to her office to get her gear and go to her truck where Les was waiting.

As she backed out of her parking space, she asked, "Well, Partner, are you ready for another exciting day?"

"If it's all the same to you, I'd like to go back to fighting with bears. There's less tension."

"Pour me some coffee and I'll see what we can do about that today."

It was a beautiful day and the drive to the ferry landing was pleasant. Gayle was in the parking area waiting with a smile on her face.

"What are you so happy about, Gayle?" asked Holden.

"Oh, nothing," she lied. "We just heard you two made another rescue last evening. Congratulations guys."

"It was kinda out of my skill range, but Les did a heck of a job. I think it might even get him an attaboy." She was chuckling, and the two lady officers held up their coffee cups in a toast to Goddard.

"I may have some news for you with regard to the big brown bear you've been watching."

"Did you spot him?" asked Holden.

"No, but we had some reports of a very large brown bear at the bear's fishing hole late last night. He was alone and stayed in the water most of the time he was out there. If you go down there you might look for his tracks," Gayle reported.

"Oh, gosh, I hope it's him. We sort of lost track of him when he went up the mountain. If it's him, we can sit on a log and watch him eat tourists." Holden was teasing her friend.

Gayle laughed, "The report we got was that even the fishermen on the other side of the river left the water to watch him."

Betty turned to Les, "Cut a fresh willow stick and let's go bear hunting."

Again, the ferry was at maximum capacity as they crossed to the other side. Again, they checked licenses and counted stringers as they made their way downstream to the fishing hole. It was well past noon when they reached their favorite observation spot. It was time to eat lunch and keep an eye on the fishermen across the river.

Les slipped off the log and rested his head where he had been sitting, "Wake me up if anything happens," he said, pulling his hat over his eyes.

Holden sipped her last cup of coffee and watched the tourists fishing on the other side of the river. It was nearly time to head back to the ferry. Les had dug his camera from his pack and was taking photos of everything in sight when he noticed several fishermen pointing to this side and moving away from the water.

"Hey, Holden," he whispered, "I think we have a visitor."

She turned around to see what was happening just as the big bear meandered toward the river. He walked slowly, keeping an eye on the fishermen on the other side. Les was snapping pictures, using his long telephoto lens.

"Oh, I don't believe this," said Goddard in surprise.

"What is it, Les?' asked Holden.

"Look with your binoculars at the crowd on the side of the highway. The one with the binoculars watching the bear," he said, still holding his camera on the spot.

Betty panned the crowd with her field glasses, "Oh, WAIT! I see him. Isn't that our old friend Burt Donnigan?"

"It sure looks like him to me. I have several pictures of him."

"Now, what do you suppose he's doing down here?" she wondered out loud. "Do you think he's just admiring the bear, or do you think he's making another plan?"

"That's the $64,000 question," commented Les. "I can't believe he's crazy enough to make another try to get this bear."

They watched Donnigan for another several minutes before Holden reached for her radio to call Sergeant Ted Wilson.

"Sarge, this is Holden," she said into the radio.

"Go ahead, Holden, what's the problem?"

"We've just seen Burt Donnigan on the other side of the river with binoculars watching the big brown bear in the fishing hole. He's not breaking any laws, but it seems strange to me that he's even here. He's really intent on watching the animal. Should we call someone to come and question him, or just watch him?" asked Holden.

There was a short silence, "Good question, Holden. If he's not breaking any laws, I guess we should only watch him. I don't want to violate any of his rights, but I don't want to ignore his curiosity either. He lost his right to hunt, but he still has the right to look. There really isn't anything we can do unless he shows up with a weapon. I guess we just watch him for now. Be sure to note the times you spotted him and the time he leaves the area." The Sergeant was as frustrated with the situation as his field personnel.

"Got it, Sarge," she said as she returned the radio to her zipper pocket.

She turned to Les, "You heard the man, we just watch him for now."

Still holding the binoculars to her eyes, she scanned the rest of the crowd. "I don't see any of his partners in the onlookers. The only one I recognize is Burt. So," she said with frustration in her voice, "I guess we watch him until the bear leaves the fishing hole."

The bear continued to catch and eat salmon for more than an hour before he climbed the high bank and returned to the woods above the river. When he was gone the crowd on the highway began to dissipate. Burt was the last of the viewers to leave the roadside. He'd watched the bear climb the embankment and wander into the woods. He was so intent on the bear he failed to see the two officers only a few yards upstream concealed in the brush. Once the bear was gone, Burt walked back in the direction of the public parking lot on the other side of the highway. The officers recognized his pickup as it drove back in the direction of Anchorage.

"Let's get back to the office, Les. I want you to make copies of those pictures of the bear and of 'Old Burt' watching it. I don't know how I'm going to write this up in my report. I guess I just put it all in there and let someone else make that determination."

They hiked upstream and crossed on the ferry. It took an hour to get back to the office and another hour to finish her report. Les had printed the photos and left copies on her desk before he left the office.

"0500 tomorrow?" he asked as he left.

"0500," she said, still writing.

The following morning the two officers were passing the bear's fishing hole and there were already two bears in the water. One of them was the big brownie. She stopped her truck to watch him for a few minutes. Only a few folks were on the edge of the road this early in the morning.

"I guess we should go to work," she said, finally.

Again, Gayle was waiting in the parking lot. "You're late," she said.

"Yeah, we stopped at the fishing hole to watch two bears catching fish. One of them was the big guy."

"I heard he was there last night. Everyone who reported it was impressed with the size of him."

"We saw him fishing last night and, we saw the poacher Burt Donnigan on the side of the road watching it. When he left, we saw him in his old pickup." She opened her notebook, "This is his license plate number. I'd appreciate it if you'd have the local Trooper keep an eye out for this truck. I want to know if he comes back to watch the bear. So far, he's only watched, but we don't know what he plans to do; just watch or plan a hunt."

They crossed the river and checked licenses and visited with the fishermen. The number of people fishing had slowed some, but it was still crowded on the riverbanks. The fishermen were having good luck with catching limits as the run continued to be strong. The weather continued to stay pleasant and the fishermen, for the most part, were in a good mood.

As they continued downstream, checking bag limits and licenses, they found only one fisherman without a license and only one fisherman over limit by twice the allowable limit of six. Both were cited and the fish taken from the overlimit offender. Les had taken the fish back to the truck to place them in a cooler, with a large bag of ice inside. He returned to join Holden as she continued to check fishermen in the river.

It was noon when they reached the bear's fishing hole and sat on their log to eat their lunches. When she finished her sandwich and soft drink for lunch, Holden began to scan the fishermen on the other side of the river. There were only a few.

"You know, Partner," she muttered while looking through her binoculars. "If Burt doesn't come back and if the bear hasn't shown himself by early afternoon, I think we can go home early and

perhaps you can get some flying time in before
you go home."

"That sounds great to me. I'll call Roger
when we start our walk back to the ferry if we do
that." The prospect of flying today excited him.

An hour later a small black bear came to the
fishing hole, but only stayed a short while. He had
caught several salmon and possibly eaten his fill
before leaving the river.

Not long after the black bear left, a nice size
bear arrived to begin fishing for his meal. It
looked like a female to Betty. Each time a bear
came to the fishing hole the crowd on the highway
side would gather to watch. Most were careful,
but some wandered into traffic, causing drivers to
dodge them and honk their horns. By late
afternoon the scene was very quiet and Holden
decided it was time to call it a day.

Another Wildlife Trooper was at the landing
when they returned. It was Don Lewis checking
bag limits of the fishermen returning to the parking
area.

"Hi, Don," Holden greeted as she stepped
off the ferry. "Have you heard how our patient's
doing?"

"Only that they're keeping him sedated until
his blood levels get somewhere close to normal.
He had another surgery and they closed up the hole
in his abdomen. And they set his leg. He needed
to have some metal plates and screws in his leg,

but the hospital told me he'd be able to hike again once it heals."

"Wow, Don. You have a newer update than we do. I'm glad he's doing well."

"I have to hand it to that partner of yours, Holden. I've never seen a backpack for live meat before," he was laughing, "But that one certainly did the job." He held out a hand to Les, "Let me shake your hand young man. You did a wonderful job, and you have my thanks."

"How long are you going to be here counting fish?" asked Holden.

"Not much longer. The word gets passed around quickly when I start checking fishermen at the ferry crossing." Don gave a quick wave and moved to check another fisherman.

Les tossed his backpack into the rear seat of the truck and climbed into the front seat.

"I don't want you to think I don't like my job, but I'm excited about learning to fly and I'm anxious to get into the airplane," he said as Holden started the engine.

"You've earned it, Partner" she complimented him as she drove onto the Sterling Highway.

CHAPTER 25

Holden chuckled as she drove toward Soldotna and glanced at the passenger seat. Les had fallen asleep, his chin on his chest. They were entering the Soldotna City Limits when she awakened Goddard. He finally was awake enough to realize where he was.

"Do you suppose you could drop me off at the airplane?" he asked in a still sleepy voice.

"Sure, that's no problem. But how are you going to get back to the office and your vehicle?"

"A friend of mine is on the Soldotna Police Department. I can call him to drive me back to the office. I'll do my daily report when I return from my flight. The weather is good, and I think I'll just go out over the Moose Range and practice some maneuvers. Then I should come back here and do some touch and goes. After all, I'm still learning these things."

"OK, Les, you know what you're doing. I'll drop you at the airport. Have a good flight and have some fun."

When they arrived at the airplane he jumped out and took his backpack from the rear seat and tossed it into the rear seat of the Super Cub. Betty waved at him and drove away to return to the office and make her own report.

She was alone in the office with no distractions, and it took only a short time to finish the report. Once done, she reached into a drawer to get the stack of printed photos of the huge brown bear. The pictures were very clear, and she could see the wet hair on the side of the big bear after he had been fighting with the smaller bear at the fishing hole. There were nearly thirty photos, and she studied each one carefully. This was a truly huge bear. He'd proven himself to be a healthy and strong animal. His hide was full and uniform in color. He was beautiful. She returned the photos to the drawer and filed her report. It was late and she only wanted to go home, have some dinner and relax for a while. They had walked many miles today and her body ached.

She entered the office at 0430 the following morning and filled her thermos bottle as well as her travel cup. She collected a handful of shotgun shells to be stashed in her backpack and was about to leave the office when Ted Wilson arrived. They met in the parking lot.

"Good morning, Sarge," she greeted as he climbed out of his truck.

"Good morning, Holden," he said. "Have you got a minute to come to my office?"

"Sure, Boss, just let me put this stuff in my truck." She walked to her State vehicle and put her shotgun and thermos in the back seat. She carried her travel cup back inside the building and to Sarge's office.

"Have a seat Betty," he said as she entered. "I have an update on the fellow you two carried out of the woods on Mystery Creek."

"I talked with Lewis at the ferry landing, and he told me the patient was improving." She volunteered.

"That was what I was told. He still has severe wounds that need more attention, but he is recovering. They're going to allow him to awaken this morning." Wilson removed his cap and ran his finger through his thinning hair. "I want to personally commend you and Les for what you did out there. I plan to do the same for Lewis, too. That citizen wouldn't have stood a chance if it hadn't been for the three of you being so innovative."

She smiled and said, "All the innovations were done by Les. He ran back to the truck, made a soft bed in the back, re-modeled his backpack and ran back up the trail to help us load the hiker on his make-shift carriage. He packed the man on his back while Lewis and I kept pressure in his wound to stop the bleeding. Les Goddard was the hero in that process."

"I'll mention all that to the Colonel when I meet with him." He was making a note on his calendar as he spoke.

"Les should be waiting out front for me, Boss. I guess I should get to work. Do you want us to do the same as yesterday?" she asked.

"Yes, and I want you to keep an eye open for Burt Donnigan while you're out there. Somehow, I don't feel good about you seeing him there at the fishing hole."

"For what it's worth, Sarge, I feel the same way." She stood and left the office to meet with her partner Les at the truck.

"How was your flight yesterday?" she asked as she climbed behind the steering wheel.

"It was great. I did some required maneuvers and practiced some landings. I called Roger and he said I only need a few more hours before I can take a check ride for my Private Pilot Certificate."

"I don't want to sound like your mother, but just be careful out there," said Holden.

The ferry was returning when they arrived and there was no Gayle to greet them. She must have been given a day off, thought Holden. They crossed the river and began to walk downstream, checking licenses and counting stringers.

It was afternoon by the time they reached the bear's fishing hole. It seemed the fishermen were behaving themselves this morning. They'd only written one citation for someone fishing without a license and he wasn't a visitor. He was a local from Cooper Landing. The officers sat on their favorite log to eat some lunch and watch fishermen on the other side of the river, near the highway.

"How was your flight last night, Les?" asked Holden in a low tone.

"It was great," answered Les, in a near whisper. "I flew up this direction to see if I could see any animals, but I didn't see much. A couple of moose downstream. The boats were thick in the canyon and the tourists looked as if they were having a great time."

"How were your flight tricks? Did they all go as planned?"

"Yes, they did. I practiced for almost two hours." He was silent for a few seconds before continuing. "I did see one strange thing, though."

"Oh, yeah, what was that?" she asked.

"You know that little campground where we busted Burt and his friends?" he said looking directly into her eyes.

"Sure, the one below Jim's Landing."

"That's the one. I was flying near the mountain on this side of the river and came across a camp in the trees. It had a small rubber raft, covered with some brush and leaves behind it. I didn't see anyone at the camp, but I thought it was a strange place to camp for fishing. The tent was a small pop-up style, only good for one man. It was also camo color. I thought at the time this guy looked more like a hunter than a fisherman."

She spoke in a normal volume, "How far downriver from here did you see the camp?" she asked.

"Hmm, maybe three miles," he replied.

"Grab your pack and let's go down there and check it out." She was already slipping into the straps of her own pack.

"What are you thinking, Holden?" he asked as he slipped into his pack.

"What if that really was a hunter?" she said, "What if our old friend Burt decided to get a closer look at the big brown bear. We know he was in the area the other day and he was watching the big bear at the fishing hole. He may have just decided to cross the river again and look for the big brownie. It would mean he has a vehicle here somewhere and I can ask Lewis to drive to Jim's Landing to look for it when he gets a few minutes."

With their packs loaded on their backs, they walked parallel to the river until they came upon the bear trail in the woods. They had checked their shotguns for a load in the chamber when they reached the bear trail.

"Follow me down the trail but keep back about five yards," she ordered. "We don't want him or the bear getting us both with one blow."

"Good thinking," said Les in a low tone.

At the slow pace they chose to take through the woods, it took nearly two hours to get near the spot where Goddard had seen the tent.

"There it is, over there in the brush," said Les.

"You stay here and cover me. I'm going to check the tent to see if anyone's there and if they left any identification." Holden knew this was a very dangerous situation but couldn't ask her partner to do this dangerous task.

She quietly moved away from the trail and toward the tent in the brushy spot where they could see the tent. Slowly she made her way to the camp. When she neared the tent, she could see the small rubber raft hidden behind it. There were faint boot prints in front of the tent where it looked as if the owner had turned around to zip up the fly.

Reaching for the zipper pull, she opened it a few inches, enough to see there was no one inside. She walked around the tent to see if she could find any tracks she could follow. Only occasional depressions were found in the foliage covered ground. She motioned for Goddard to join her.

When he got close, she whispered, "It's late in the day and I want to stake out this tent. I'm thinking we could hide down the slope over there in the thick brush. We'd be able to see anyone returning to the tent without being seen ourselves. If it turns out to be Burt, I want you to cover me when I identify myself. He's lost his privilege to hunt, and he may get testy when he sees me. He's a professional hunter and we may not hear him coming back, so stay alert. You stay here and keep your eyes open. I'm going over to that little knoll and wait. It gets dark this time of year, in about three hours. We'll have to be back on familiar ground before then. That means we can only wait about an hour and a half."

Goddard nodded and stepped behind a huge willow bush to watch. Holden made her way through the trees and brush to the little hill a few yards from the front of the tent where she began her wait for the owner. Time passed slowly with only the far-off sound of the river and the rustling sounds of squirrels in the woods. There were many types of birds in the foliage, and it should have been a peaceful and serene wait, but the tension was severe. Holden couldn't see her partner who was waiting only a few yards to her right.

They waited for more than an hour and a half when Holden stood to call to her partner, "Come over and get a few pictures of this camp, Les. We're going to need to make the hike back as quickly as we can. It won't be pitch dark when we get to the ferry crossing, but it's going to be late."

Les quickly took about twenty pictures of the camp from many angles. When he had finished storing his camera in his pack, he said, "OK, partner, let's go home."

The hike back upstream went much faster than the one they had made earlier. With a steady pace they were back at the crossing in just over two hours. The sun was behind the mountains, and it was setting across the inlet. Darkness was setting in quickly.

They had begun the drive back to Soldotna when Holden remembered she hadn't talked with Lewis about checking the campground for Burt Donnigan's truck.

"I think I'll take a short jaunt to Jim's Landing to look for Burt's truck. If it's not there, we'll swing into that trailhead on Skilak Loop to see if he left it there."

"Sounds like a good idea to me, Partner," replied Les.

They checked both places with no sign of the truck.

"I guess I could be wrong about 'old Burt' being the owner of the camp on the other side," said Holden in a sad voice. "But the way the camp was hidden, I would have sworn it was Donnigan looking for the bear. I guess we'll have to discuss it with the boss in the morning.

Ted Wilson's truck was in the parking lot when they returned to the office. Inside she stopped at his office and asked him for permission to speak with him.

"Come on in, both of you. You're out a little late tonight, aren't you?"

"Yes, and we're tired from all the hiking we had to do today," began Holden. "Les was flying last night and spotted a camp downriver from Jim's Landing. It struck me that, since we'd seen Burt Donnigan in the area, it could be him setting up a bear hunting camp across the river. We hiked down there and found the camp. Les has some pictures of the place. We staked it out and waited until we thought we'd better get out before it got dark and wouldn't be able to see the trail. I just wanted to check to see if you have any ideas as to how to go about watching that camp. We didn't find Burt's truck, and that got me thinking it could be someone else. The camp doesn't look like and isn't in a place where a fisherman would be camped. Do you have any ideas?" She turned to Les, "Show him the photos, Partner."

Les brought the digital pictures to the small screen and passed the camera to the Sergeant.

"Holy smokes, Holden. I think you did the right thing. Let me think about it until morning and I may be able to get you some help with this. Now, go home and get some rest. It's pretty late right now. Come in at 0900 tomorrow and I'll have some word for you."

CHAPTER 26

It was only 0800 when Holden parked in front of the office and entered to check in with her boss. "Good morning, Boss," she said as she approached his door.

He looked up and then checked his watch, "Aren't you a little early?"

"A little, I guess. I wanted to see if you had any ideas about what to do with that tent camp we discussed."

"Let's get a cup of coffee and we can talk about it." He stood and motioned for her to follow him to the break room where he poured two cups of coffee and sat at one of the small tables.

"I have to admit you've given me a big problem. I thought about it all night and I've decided this is a problem worth investing man hours into. I want you two to continue your bear watch duties. I'm going to assign two undercover officers to watch the camp. They'll pose as fishermen and make a sleeping camp on the riverbank in the area of that tent. They'll watch out for the owner of the tent and try to learn who he is and what he's doing there. They'll have their own boat, but as you know, no motor, only oars. Whomever is out there in the woods will have to come back to the camp sooner or later." Ted removed his cap and rubbed his head.

"It sounds like a good idea, Sarge. Les and I'll be working in the area above them and within radio distance if they need backup. I don't know who you're sending out there, but I hope you warn them about Burt. This camp may not belong to him, but I'm betting it's his."

"This bear has cost us a lot of man hours, but I think this bear is worth the effort. I contacted the Colonel and he reluctantly agreed with me on this one. He's sending us two men from up North, from the Yukon area, I think. They should be flying into Soldotna sometime this morning. I'll have them contact you when they get into the area, and you can give them instructions as to how to get to the campsite. Try not to meet them face to face, just give them info on the radio."

Holden chuckled, "It sounds like you're taking this bear personally, Sarge."

"Maybe I am." He said, "I've seen this bear and he's exceptional. We don't want to lose him to a poacher."

After her meeting with the Sarge, she gathered her gear and loaded it into the truck. Les had already put his pack in the rear seat and was sitting on the passenger side when she climbed into the driver's seat.

"Mornin' Betty," he said, still sipping his cup of coffee.

"Good morning to you, too, Les," she answered.

They were out of town when Les asked, "Well, what's the detail for today?"

"Same old thing, but the Sarge sent a couple undercover officers to watch the bear. All we have to do is check licenses and watch the fishing hole," She replied.

"Dang, I love this job," he replied, grinning and sipping more coffee.

"It looks like we have banker's hours today. We can make the walk downstream, check the fishermen and finally have lunch at the bear's fishing hole. I guess we have nothing to worry about unless we hear gunshots downstream and need to see who, or what, got shot." It was an indication she wanted to be in the woods checking on the big bear.

Gayle was waiting at the ferry landing when they arrived.

"How do you know what time we're going to be here?" asked Holden.

"I have spies everywhere," said Gayle with a short laugh.

"It's nice to know someone cares," replied Betty.

"Well, Lewis and I want to get with you this afternoon and buy you dinner. You can pick the place, but we wanted you to know we appreciate you guys a lot."

"Thanks, Gayle. You know Les and I'll go anywhere for food."

"You pick the spot. Where do you want to go for dinner?" insisted Gayle.

Betty looked at Les, "What do you think, Partner? Sunrise?"

"That would be great with me," he replied,

"There you go, Gayle. I'll call you on the radio when we head back upriver."

The ferry returned and the officers crossed once again to begin their walk and check fishermen. Shortly after noon they arrived at their favorite log to eat lunch.

About the same time they were sitting down to eat lunch, two men with rifles and fishing gear were catching a drift boat in Cooper Landing for a float trip downstream to Jim's Landing. There, the other fishermen would be transported back to the boat launch in town. These two men had asked to be dropped off on the other side of the river, where they intended to fish and camp. The drift boat captain advised them against it because of bears in the area, but they wouldn't listen, replying they'd do this at their own risk.

The men, undercover officers, were dropped on the riverbank a short distance above Jim's Landing, below where Betty and Les were having lunch. They immediately rigged their fishing rods and began to cast for Sockeye Salmon. They fished for an hour and a half before leaving the water to find a camping spot. They contacted Holden and Goddard by radio at the bear's fishing hole. They agreed to walk toward each other to meet and discuss the situation.

As they met, the new officers made a show of presenting their licenses to the uniformed officers.

"I'm Ned Bishop and this is my partner, Loren Daws. Sergeant Wilson said you'd be here to meet with us. We've been briefed on the general problem, but we need to know if there's anything special for us to look out for."

"Well, Ned, I can think of two things for you to be aware of. First is the bear. He's around eleven feet tall and thinks he owns the entire river. Second is a poacher by the name of Burt Donnigan. We don't know if he's the one who owns the tent camp in the woods downstream, but he's the most likely suspect. I think you've already read the reports and I won't go into that, but this man could be dangerous. He's a hunting guide and he's comfortable in the woods."

"Thanks for the warning. Can you give us a better position for the tent? Neither of us has been down here before and I can see the radio contact is going to be limited," Ned was still doing the talking.

"There are some other things to think about. You don't have a boat and the only way to cross the river is upstream about three miles or more. Radio contact is sketchy and the chances of summoning help in an emergency are almost nonexistent. Les and I'll be working in the area during the day, but only from here to the ferry, and on foot. We can't guarantee a quick response."

She paused a moment, "I guess what I'm trying to say is, be on guard at all times. If the camp does belong to Old Burt, he could be dangerous to you."

"We understand, Officer Holden, and thank you for your concerns."

The new officers made careful notes of the directions to the camp site and bid Holden and Goddard farewell.

It was getting late when Holden turned to Les and said she thought it was time to head back to the ferry. An hour later they were back in the parking lot at the ferry landing. She sat in the front seat of her truck to make some notes in her logbook before starting the engine. It was after five o'clock in the afternoon and both officers were ready for some dinner. Traffic was heavy and slow as they drove up the highway toward the Sunrise Inn.

"Grab my radio and call Gayle to see if she and Lewis are at the restaurant yet," she said to Les.

The reply was that the other two officers were there and waiting for them. Gayle and Lewis had gone inside to get a table by the time they arrived. Holden wanted to go inside and sit down after the long day of hiking. Gayle waved at the two as they entered.

As Holden sat, she gave a long, contented sigh. "I must be getting old," she said, taking a seat. "I used to be able to go for days without stopping, and now here I am pooped out with only nine hours under my belt."

"I thought you were getting younger," said Lewis. "After all, I saw you and Les in action up on Mystery Creek. I don't think there's a recruit on the force that can keep up with you."

"I didn't do much on that deal. You and Les did all the work," she said as the waitress came with menus.

"What would you like to drink?" she asked.

Each ordered Iced Tea and sipped the tall glasses as they waited.

"I met those two undercover officers downstream this afternoon. They seem to know what they're doing. You may want to keep an ear out for a radio call from them. They appear to be experienced, but they're out there alone and may need some help at some point." Betty was passing on confidential information to her coworkers.

When dinner was finished, Betty and Les drove back to the office to file their reports. At the same time, the undercover officers had made a camp with a plastic tarp and some sticks to form a lean-to shelter. Once that was done, they strolled around the vicinity to see if they could find any bear tracks or tracks of the hunter. The summer foliage was green and lush and almost no tracks of any kind could be seen. They found the bear trail and followed it to where they thought the camp was located, finding it without much trouble. They watched the camp for a long time from a short distance away, hidden in the trees and brush to avoid being seen.

Finally, Daws leaned close to Bishop and whispered, "Do you think this is a dummy camp meant to throw us off the trail?"

"Good thinking, Loren. How about you stay here, and I go take a closer look at the camp?"

Daws nodded agreement.

Bishop made a retreat back into the woods to circle around and make a direct path to the tent. As he approached, he noted there hadn't been anyone near the camp for several days. He checked the tent and the camp for signs, but it hadn't had anyone in it in recent days.

He left the area in the same direction he had entered from. Again, he circled to return to where Daws was hidden.

"I think you're right, Loren. It looks like a dummy camp. No one's been there for several days. Let's make a wide circle up and around the camp, go up the mountain and see if we can come across some recent tracks?"

"He could be watching this camp, so we should take care and make a very wide circle around," Daws noted.

The men carefully left the site to begin a circuitous path to higher points on the mountain. It was very slow going, but eventually they climbed above the tree line. In the willows, high on the hillside, they located a camouflaged campsite. Someone had dug a shallow depression in the dirt, lined it with plastic tarp and placed a high-quality sleeping bag there. They covered the entire site with another brown tarp, which was covered with small branches of brush and leaves as disguise.

"Someone has been using this camp," said Loren,

"Try to avoid leaving any tracks or sign we've been here. Do you see that heavy patch of brush over there about a hundred yards?" he pointed to the spot.

Ned Bishop nodded, "I see it," he said.

"I think we can build a small campsite over there and keep an eye on this one. At least we might learn exactly who we're dealing with."

"If this guy is hunting the bear and not fishing, I think he'll be back here sometime around dark. Let's get busy before he decides to come back," replied Ned.

Once more, the officers made a wide circle to the observation spot they had chosen. It had been an easy task to build a comfortable place to wait for the hunter to return.

"Have you seen any bear tracks up here?" asked Loren.

"No I haven't, but it may be the reason he built his camp in this location."

The men settled in to wait for the hunter to return. It was nearly dark when Loren poked Ned. "Someone's coming to the other camp," he whispered.

Both men watched with binoculars as the man carefully approached his camp on the hillside. He stopped for a long while to study the camp before approaching it, crawling into the sleeping bag in the depression.

"Did you get a good look at him?" asked Ned.

"Not really good, but I think he's the same one we have the photograph of. The one taken by that young temp, Les."

Loren spoke softly again, "This guy's packing a rifle and no fishing rod. That tells me we have the right man. He hasn't done anything for us to arrest him for, so you watch him for a couple of hours and wake me up and I'll watch for a while. We can try to follow him in the morning. I really think he'll be up and at 'em by daylight."

CHAPTER 27

It was very early in the day and the sun had not yet reached high enough to cast rays even this far down the mountain. Loren and Ned kept to the brushy patches above the trail the hunter was taking to get to the wooded area below.

They'd followed the hunter for more than two miles when he stopped and bent down to look at something on the trail. "He may have spotted a bear track," whispered Ned.

Loren nodded agreement as they continued to follow him down the trail toward the river. The hunter was following a well-used game trail down the mountainside. When the hunter vanished into the trees of the wooded area, Ned leaned close and whispered, "Let's give him a few minutes, then follow him into the trees. We should be able to get closer to him down there. It's going to be tougher to see his tracks when we get into the woods. Keep your eyes open."

A few minutes later the officers slowly made their way to the edge of the woods. Inside the tree cover they became a team with Ned following the tracks and Loren keeping an eye out for the hunter. Slowly the pair eased down the trail, following the man ahead of them. They'd been successful staying out of sight of the hunter who was intent on following some tracks he kept checking on the leaf covered trail.

Ahead there was the sound of branches breaking. The hunter stopped and cautiously peered into the trees, moving only a few feet at a time. Each time they lost sight of the hunter, Ned motioned for Loren to follow him. They kept a low profile and walked down the trail behind the hunter, attempting to do it without making a sound.

The hunter had now become very intent on the sounds ahead of him on the trail. He stepped only inches at a time, stopping with each step to survey the area in front of him.

Moments later there was another crackling of the brush downhill from the men. Again, the hunter became more cautious, bending low to be less visible in the foliage. A few yards later the hunter bent down again to look at something on the trail. Then he moved again, and the officers lost sight of him.

They waited for almost a minute before moving toward his position. As he had done, they bent low to be less visible in the low brush and ferns along the trail. They could hear the water rippling in the river not far away.

As they moved down the trail, Ned stopped to point out a pile of fresh bear scat on the path. Loren nodded and the two moved on cautiously. When they neared the lower edge of the trees, they saw the hunter crouched in the grass. Ned motioned for Loren to crouch even lower against the trail.

The hunter was sliding his rifle from his shoulder as he kneeled on the trail. Ned did the same as he motioned for Loren to take a position behind one of the nearby trees. Quietly, Loren did as he was instructed and eased his rifle from his shoulder, carefully easing the safety off.

The officers were watching the drama ahead of them when there was a sudden movement on the trail. The hunter raised his rifle to fire and waited for the animal to come into view.

There was a huffing sound in the grass and brush ahead and suddenly a giant brown bear stood up on his hind legs only a few yards from the hunter.

The hunter turned slightly to aim when Ned shouted, "HOLD IT, don't shoot."

The sound startled the bear who dropped to all fours and turned to run.

The hunter fired a shot after the bear, but the distraction had caused him to pull off the target. Without hesitation the hunter turned the rifle in the direction of Ned Bishop.

"That's not a good idea, mister," shouted Loren from behind the tree. "Put the gun down and put your hands on the top of your head."

"What the.." shouted the hunter.

"I said drop the weapon and do it now," Loren ordered again.

The hunter realized he was dealing with two men, not just the one he could see.

"OK, OK," he said as he pointed the muzzle skyward and slipped the safety on before gently laying the weapon on the ground and raising his hands to the top of his head. He could see the barrel of the weapon in the area of the voice.

Ned moved closer and picked up the hunter's rifle while pointing his own at the hunter. Loren moved closer and took the hunter's rifle from him. He lay both his and the hunters' rifles on the grass near the trail before moving closer to step behind the hunter, grasping his left wrist to apply a set of handcuffs. Once the hunter was secured, Ned lowered his rifle and gave a long sigh of relief.

The angry hunter was now becoming defensive.

"How come you're treating me like this. You must have seen the bear attacking me" he shouted at the officers.

Ned only smiled, "What's your name, mister?" he asked.

"I'm Burt Donnigan," he replied in an angry tone.

"Well, Mr. Donnigan, we didn't see you being attacked by the bear, but if we stay here much longer, he may come back and finish the job." Ned spoke as he took a plastic card from his shirt pocket. Let me read you your rights while I get my breath." He read the card to Burt, "Do you understand these rights?" he asked.

Donnigan nodded without saying anything.

"Loren, would you take a look inside Mr. Donnigan's backpack to see if there are any more weapons inside?"

"Sure thing, Ned," he replied as he stepped up behind Burt and opened his pack. He rummaged around inside and found nothing except a large hunting knife which he removed and stuffed inside Ned's pack. He nodded to Ned that it was clear.

"OK now, Mr. Donnigan, we have a very long walk back up the river to the ferry crossing. I want you to behave. Where's your hunting license?"

"I don't have one," said the angry Burt.

Loren chuckled, "I didn't see any fishing gear in your pack and no camera either. You were holding a rifle and aiming at a bear. I think you were out here hunting."

Ned intervened, "OK, boys, that's enough fun. We have a long walk ahead. Loren, you take the lead, I'll take the rear and keep an eye on the prisoner. I can carry his rifle. You break trail and keep anyone we meet away from the prisoner. I'll get on the radio as soon as I can get a signal to have someone meet us at the ferry crossing."

"You guys are making a big mistake. I'm going to sue you and your department for your jobs and a lot of money. You endangered my life by taking my rifle." An irate Donnigan was nearly shouting now.

"Don't you worry, Burt, we'll take good care of the rifle for you. Now, start walking back to the ferry landing.

They had moved about two miles upstream when they encountered Goddard and Holden on the riverbank. The arresting officers waved at them as they were checking licenses. Holden immediately recognized Donnigan and stepped back up to the trail to meet the small group. Burt was still angry and protesting. His hands were handcuffed behind him, and he was obviously uncomfortable. The three men stopped to talk with the two officers. Loren remained a few steps behind the group.

"What have you got here, Officer Bishop?" asked Holden.

"I know you know this man. I know how you admire him. But, we had to arrest him when he attempted to shoot a very large brown bear. He claims self-defense, but we witnessed the act and didn't see it as he swears it was." Bishop was holding the chain of the handcuffs tightly, preventing him from attempting to run.

Holden turned to Burt, "Why Mr. Donnigan, I remember you telling the judge you were through with this bear. Shame on you."

"I'll show you who has the shame. I'm suing all of you for false arrest and harassment. Let's see how funny it is when I get you to court."

Ned interrupted the banter with a question of his own, "Say, Holden. Do you have a signal here? I can't seem to contact anyone on my radio."

"It's a dead spot right here. The hills block the signal on these small hand radios. Come on. Les and I'll walk with you up to the crossing. We'll be able to contact them from about the halfway point."

"Good. We're going to need a transport officer. We don't have a vehicle here," said Bishop.

"I'll call it in as soon as we get into radio range," Holden informed the newcomers.

The four officers and the prisoner began the walk up the river trail toward the ferry crossing. A mile upstream Holden was able to contact the office and relay what had taken place. Ted Wilson came on the air to say he was sending a Trooper to meet them at the ferry landing.

"Is everyone safe?" asked Wilson.

"Yessir, Boss. We're all fine. Burt's in custody and complaining, so I know he's OK too. Les and I'll be following the Trooper back to town and we'll report to the office as soon as the prisoner's delivered."

"Good. I want to congratulate those new men on a job well done. Burt's a dangerous man, in my opinion. See you when you get to town."

Holden turned to Bishop and asked, "How would you boys like a cup of hot coffee when we get across the river?"

"I'll look forward to that," said Loren from rear of the parade.

Betty changed the channel on the radio to contact Gayle, "Hey, Gayle. It's Betty. I have a couple officers here that missed their morning coffee. Do you have any to spare?"

"Sure do, a fresh thermos full. Are you crossing the river?" she asked.

"About a half hour or so," Holden replied. "The Sarge is sending a Trooper to take the prisoner to Kenai. We'll be waiting there."

"I just ordered you guys some coffee," she said as she stuffed the radio back inside the zipper pocket.

As the little ferry came ashore, Holden motioned for the operator to come and talk with her. She asked for special seats for the five of them on this trip across the river. The operator agreed to seat them where they'd be the first to step off the little boat when they reached the other side of the river. The crossing takes less than five minutes on a normal day, and this was a very normal day for the operator.

Gayle was waiting when they arrived. Loren and Ned helped Burt to get seated on the tailgate of Gayle's truck. They didn't offer him any of the coffee she poured for the officers. He expressed his displeasure for their disregard of etiquette.

It was Officer Lewis who came to pick up the prisoner. He gladly had a cup of coffee with the officers while getting instructions as to what to do with the poacher. Once the coffee had been consumed, Loren and Ned assisted Burt in getting into the rear seat of the patrol car. It had a wire cage behind the front seat and the officers removed his handcuffs for a more comfortable ride.

"Come on you two, we'll follow Lewis to Kenai and let you see them book him in. The booking officer will want some information about the arrest and your ID numbers. After that we'll come back to the office to meet with Sergeant Wilson."

"Sounds good to me," said Bishop, with Loren Daws nodding agreement.

When they arrived at the jail complex, Lewis went through the electronic gate to enter the sallyport where prisoners were taken into the booking area. Inside, Lewis signed for the prisoner and turned him over to jail personnel.

Bishop and Daws left their weapons in the truck with Holden and Goddard while they entered the secure area to meet with the booking officers. It took only a few minutes to finish the booking and for them to come back to the truck. Holden drove directly to the office where the Sarge was waiting.

Wilson was waiting inside when they arrived and asked them to meet with him in the little break room. The long table with chairs made a more comfortable place to hear the report.

When they were seated, Wilson stood, smiled and said, "I want you to know how proud I am of this entire squad. You accomplished a miracle without anyone being injured. I congratulate you all. I know you'll each submit a report, but right now I'd like to hear exactly what took place."

Ned Bishop began the narration. He and Loren Daws related the entire episode to the Sergeant.

When they finished, Wilson asked, "Then the bear is still out there, is that right?"

"He sure is, Sarge. I want you to know he's a big one. The last time we saw him he was leaving the gunfight on a full run. We can't say if he is still in the area or not, but I think this big boy does whatever he wants to do without asking questions."

"I also want to thank you for that. Goddard and Holden will tell you I have a special interest in this bear because he's the largest bear I've ever seen on the Kenai Peninsula. I want him to feel free to roam this country and be a bear. We'll keep an eye on him and make sure he isn't a problem, but he didn't get this big by being nice. The first time I saw him he'd just killed a very large horse belonging to a guide and packer on the upper end of Skilak Lake. Good job, guys."

The Sergeant shook each officer's hand as they left the small break room.

CHAPTER 28

The sockeye run had peaked, and the numbers were beginning to dwindle. Many bears were still coming to the river to feed on the nutritious fishes, not only at the fishing hole, but all the way up the Kenai River and even up the Russian River. There were bear sightings along the shoreline all the way to the Russian River Falls. Gayle and her helpers had a tough time protecting the fishermen along the riverbank on the upper Russian River.

Gayle managed to keep any more fishermen from being injured by local bears. It was the time of year the bears feed without stopping, to gain as much fat as possible before they climb back up the mountain slopes to find a place to spend the winter. Much of Gayle's time was spent policing the areas where bears were feeding. She admired the bears and worked hard to keep the bears and fishermen apart.

Most fishermen fear the bears enough to leave a fishing hole when they arrive, but some take it personally and will fight the bears for the fishing spot. Usually, it turns out to be a free stringer of fish for the bears.

The Russian River is probably the most famous fishing spot in the entire world and has been for decades. In years gone by, the military would fly troops from all over the world to Anchorage and send busloads of them to the

Russian River to enjoy the spectacle. That practice ceased many years ago, but local soldiers and airmen still come here for weekend fishing nearly every year.

On the main river, the Kenai River, the bears were still coming to feed. Some places were favorites of black bears, and some places were reserved for brown bears. They seldom share fishing holes, and many fights break out when they cross paths. Brown bears are known to kill black bears at these fishing holes. For that reason, they tend to avoid each other.

Brown bears feeding on the river seldom attack fishermen, however if they take a notion to fish in any fishing hole they'll challenge a human intruder, who usually leaves without taking his stringer of fish to slow his departure.

Gayle Portman, the local Fish and Wildlife Trooper, had taken to naming this huge brown bear "Old Brownie" in all her reports. The name was now accepted by the Troopers who met the bear. For want of another moniker, Holden had adopted the name when referring to this bear.

"Old Brownie" didn't care what anyone called him, he was the king of this riverbank. He roamed the fishing holes and ate at any place he chose. He became the king and was seldom ever challenged by man or bear. The size is measured by his height and girth. His long brown fur was thick and full. His girth was growing to unimaginable size as he fed on the plentiful fish.

He was truly the largest bear ever seen on the Kenai Peninsula. "Old Brownie" truly was the king of the river.

He'd moved downstream, away from his favorite fishing hole to a spot just above the whitewater canyon below Jim's Landing. Few fishermen chose to cross to the South bank of the river for fear they would be challenged by one of these bears.

Back in the office, Sergeant Ted Wilson had rewarded Les and Betty with a much-needed day off. Holden had lots of laundry to wash and a house that needed cleaning after working all these days without the time to do chores. She slept late the first morning and dressed in a housecoat, ate breakfast and gathered her washing to put in the machine. She'd started the washer and was having her third cup of coffee when her cell phone rang. It was Sarge.

"Hi there, Holden," he greeted her. "Don't panic, I just called to let you know the judge just sent Donnigan back to jail requiring a huge bail amount. He told Burt he set the bail that high because he was already out on bail and failed to obey the laws of the State and therefore the new bail would be far greater than the first one. Donnigan threw a fit in court and was charged with disorderly conduct in addition to the other charges and the judge added another thousand dollars to the bail. He told the judge he wouldn't pay it and the judge sent him back to jail to await his trial date. I just thought you'd enjoy that bit of news."

"That is good news, Sarge. Can I get another day off?" she teased.

"As a matter of fact, you can have another day off. I'll call Goddard and tell him he has one too." His tone became more serious, "You two have done an outstanding job on this assignment, and I think you deserve the days off. Les may even like it and go flying." He said, laughing at his own statement. "See you in two days. You can go back to the Russian River and help Gayle with the mob."

"Thanks Boss," she said as she hung up the telephone.

Minutes later she received another call. It was Les. "Hi Holden." He said in a cheery voice.

"Oh, Hi Les, I guess Sarge must have called you,"

"Yes, he did, and I called Roger. He's going to give me my check ride for my private pilot license. I wanted you to be the first one I called to tell. I'm excited," he exclaimed.

"Well, good luck to you Les. Just be careful out there."

"I will, and thanks again for your support." He hung up without saying anything else.

Two days later they were back on duty and had driven to the ferry landing where Gayle was waiting. "Hi Gayle, have you been keeping the peace while we were getting rested up?"

"I sure have. We haven't shot anyone since you were here. How was your time off? Restful, I hope."

"I slept a lot and did a lot of laundry, but Les here, took his check ride and was issued a private pilot license."

"Well, congratulations Les. That's a big accomplishment. Do you plan to buy an airplane?" asked Gayle as she poured him another cup of coffee.

"I plan to get one someday, but I can't afford it right now. I'm going to the academy this fall so I guess after I get on permanently, I can start thinking about that."

"Congratulations, again, Les. I thought you were going back to college. I didn't know you were staying with the department."

"Sarge gave me a real challenge and said if I came on as a fulltime officer, he'd see that I could finish my degree online and arrange for my in-class time to be covered. He also had Roger give me flight instructions. The department has been wonderful to me, and I accepted the offer," Les stated proudly.

"I think we should go to work before the good Sergeant fires us both," said Holden.

Gayle looked at her watch and said, "I think you're right, Betty. It's getting late, and I have to get over to the campground to check on some campers." She gave them a wave of her hand and walked to her truck.

The officers rode the ferry across the river and began the long walk downstream to do their duties. There were fewer fishermen on the riverbanks today, but it was still crowded at several prime locations.

They ate lunch on their favorite log near the bear's fishing hole and watched the river to see if any bears were in the vicinity. They were surprised when a young brown bear appeared from behind them and walked directly to the river without even looking in their direction.

As the bear waded into the water below them, Les whispered to Holden, "Where the heck did he come from?"

Betty only smiled and watched. Later that afternoon it began to cloud over and threaten rain. When the small bear had gone, Holden turned to Goddard and said, "I think we can call it a day, Les."

He immediately began to pick up his belongings and put them back into his backpack. As he worked, he turned to face Holden and spoke to her, "I like the idea of leaving a little early today. I've got some paperwork to do at the office. It has to do with the hiring process, and I really need to get it all filled out and submitted."

"OK, then, Les. I'll get ready and we can leave. I'll need to do a daily report when we get to the office as well."

Once they reached the parking lot and put the packs in the back seat, Holden made a radio call to Gayle who was working in the area of the campground,

"We're going to the office a little early today, Gayle. We saw one small brown bear, but nothing else. See you tomorrow."

"OK, Betty, not much to report from here either. See you tomorrow."

An hour later they were entering the office. They worked on paperwork for more than an hour before going home for the night.

At the bear's fishing hole, the weather was darkening, and the daylight was fading. It hadn't yet begun to rain when a giant brown bear came down the trail to the fishing hole. It was "Old Brownie". He stopped on the high bank to survey the river. Seeing no intruders, he made his way down the embankment to the river's edge where he stopped again to check his surroundings. Satisfied it was safe, he entered the water and waded out a short distance to where the fish were traveling upstream. He stood quietly for a moment, then poked his head into the water and came out with a Sockeye. He carried it to shore where he bit it and ate the eggs from inside. He chewed on the rest of the fish until it was gone. He repeated the process for five more fish before calling it a day and again climbed the steep bank to leave the area in the direction of the hillside.

It was late in the evening and the weather was changing, causing the earlier fishermen to leave and the fishing hole was deserted.

Because of the impending weather change, Gayle had been called back to the campground to mediate a squabble between two campers arguing over the last available campsite.

"OK, which one of you was here first?" she asked.

"I was," said the shorter of the men. "He said I had to leave because he'd reserved this spot earlier in the day, but there's nothing posted here. We're all set up with our tents and I'm not taking them down." He was speaking in a very strong tone.

"I left my car over there to mark the spot," said the other camper, pointing to a van parked on the other side of the road.

"Did you leave a note or anything on the table here to tell someone you were going to set up here?" asked Gayle.

"No, I just left my van over there." he said, pointing his thumb at the vehicle.

"Without knowing any more than I do, I must agree with the man who has his tent pitched. You should have put something here to let others know you intended to stay in this space. You could have pitched your tent earlier and then gone fishing, but you didn't." Gayle had made her judgement.

The ousted camper became angry, "Where am I supposed to camp then?" he demanded.

"That'll be your problem, sir," replied Gayle.

The irate camper was about to say something else when Gayle stopped him. "I think now you should leave Sir. I don't want to cite you for disorderly conduct, but I will if you refuse to move on."

That seemed to stop the discussion and the man walked to his van and left the area.

"I thank you for your help, Officer," said the camper. "I don't like confrontations."

Gayle chuckled, "Neither do I," she said as she departed the area.

It was sprinkling drops of rain. It had been a very long day for this officer. She didn't enjoy breaking up these discussions and thought it was better done by the park ranger, but he wasn't on duty now because the camp was completely full. He had put signs out to inform drivers of the fact. The rain became steadily worse, and it was very late. She decided to call it a day.

CHAPTER 29

It rained the past two days and there were no reports of sightings of the big brown bear. Ted Wilson had let Holden return to the riverbank to help Gayle keep the peace along the river. She'd worked her way downstream alone and was checking licenses as she went. There were other brown bears seen at the fishing hole, but not the big brownie.

Wilson had also decided he should make an aerial survey of the entire area. He called Les to be his observer on the patrol. Les was excited to be flying with an officer who knew the river and foothills so well.

They rode in the same vehicle to the airport to preflight the little Super Cub. They found the tanks were full and the oil was topped off. All the control surfaces were working well, and they saw no damage to the aircraft in the walk-around.

Les climbed into the rear seat and strapped in while Ted climbed into the front pilot seat. There were some low clouds over the mountains and misty rain falling at intermittent intervals. Both man put on headphones to be able to talk with each other through the intercom system.

"Are you ready?" asked Wilson, pressing the intercom/radio mic button.

"Whenever you are. Sarge," replied Les, with a smile.

Ted added power to taxi across the apron. He reported his intentions on the local radio channel. At the West end of the airstrip he turned, added power and lifted off the ground in less than two hundred feet. Climbing at a steady rate he turned to the Southwest again, flying at about 500 feet above the ground. Both men looked for game animals as they covered the miles.

They noted several boats drifting the Kasilof River as they flew up the river toward Tustamena Lake. Wilson stayed over the North shore of the lake. They watched the shoreline for signs of bears and other game animals. At the upper end of the lake the pilot began to climb to a better altitude as they flew upward over the hillside and Emma Lake. With little in the way of brush or trees on this hillside it was easy to spot any animals feeding on the ridge.

On the lower reaches of the mountainside there were several moose cows with calves. Wilson took this as a good sign they would have a fair number of moose available during the coming hunting season.

From the rear seat Les spoke into the intercom, "Hey, Sarge. Look over there, above the lake. It looks like a very large black bear."

Ted banked the airplane to turn in the direction of the black bear. As they got closer, he spoke into his radio, "I'll be darned, Les, that's not a black bear, it's a very dark brown bear. I've heard this bear was living up here, but I had never seen him before. You've got good eyes, Son."

"Wow, I didn't know they could be this dark. I really thought it was a black bear."
"They come in all colors. This black one is very unusual, though. See if you can get any pictures of him while I circle wide. I don't want to frighten him."

Les lifted the camera from his lap and snapped several pictures as they flew in a wide circle around the bear.

As they left the area of this bear, they flew up the ridge toward the glacier where they spotted several caribou laying on the ice. They liked this spot to avoid mosquitoes.

"Are there a lot of caribou in this area?" asked Les.

"As a rule, we see quite a few. They were transplanted here several years ago. They mingle with the lowland animals in the fall and early winter.

It's not too hot today, but these guys lay out here to keep cool and foil the mosquitoes. I don't know why they're here today with the light rain we're encountering. Habit I guess. Let's go over the top and buzz Bill Dover's place, just for fun."

As they flew over the ridge, they spotted another nice brown bear near the brush line on the Skilak side of the mountain. Flying slowly, they were able to look carefully at the hillside and any hiding places the bears might have found.

Flying down the canyon toward the Kenai River canyon Ted said, "Les, give Holden a call on the radio and tell her we would buy her lunch at Sunrise if she can get away."

Les did as he was ordered and spoke to Holden. She agreed to meet them at the Cooper Landing Airstrip.

She was sitting in her vehicle when they parked the little Cub. Sergeant Wilson stepped out first with Les a few short seconds behind. She drove to the airplane and waited.

Wilson sat in the front seat with Holden. Les was in the rear. It was only a short drive to the restaurant. The gregarious owner was at the cash register when they entered.

"Hi, guys," she greeted as they entered. "I haven't seen you for a while. What can I get you to drink?"

They ordered iced tea and found a table in the corner of the dining room. They placed their orders and sipped the sweet tea.

"How's it going this morning, Holden?" asked the Sarge.

"It's going good, pretty slow for the fishermen, though," replied Betty.

"I'll probably pull you two back to do another detail within a few days. Gayle can manage this area now, given the numbers of fishermen is declining," said Wilson. "Have you had any reports of the big brown bear?" he inquired.

"No one had seen him in the past couple of days. I've asked some of the people I know who fish the area on a regular basis and they haven't seen him."

"Burt Donnigan has some court hearings coming up soon. I've had some calls from the DA asking me about what I want done with him. To tell you the truth, he broke his word at the last court hearing, and I don't expect him to keep it this time unless they give him some jail time to cool him down." Wilson spoke between bites of his sandwich.

Les put his sandwich back on the plate and wiped his mouth with his napkin. "You know, Sarge, I've been thinking about Burt. I'm wondering if he's in contact with his hunting buddies. It was my thought that if they went with him on the first poaching trip, he may try to get them to go it alone while he's in jail. What do you think of that idea?"

Sergeant Wilson was thinking now, "Hmmm, I never thought of that angle, but it's a good possibility. When I get back to the office I'll call and ask the jail to check the records on his phone calls."

"You know," said Holden, "You two are scary. You think way too much alike."

Wilson was smiling, "You know, Holden? I think I like this young man. Try to not get him fired while you train him." All three officers were laughing.

At the cash register the sergeant paid the bill and the owner Arden, took the cash. "Good to see you again folks. Sorry I'm so busy I didn't get a chance to visit. Perhaps next time. Bye now," she said, handing Wilson his change.

Holden drove the two pilots to the airplane and watched them climb into the little plane. This time Wilson climbed into the back seat and Les took the pilot seat. They put on their headsets and readied for takeoff. Les spoke on the radio and looked in all directions before moving the Piper into position for takeoff. A moment later they were airborne, flying back toward Soldotna.

Holden had bought an extra sandwich to take back to the ferry landing where Gayle was working. She contacted the local officer on the radio to be sure she was there and asked her to meet with her at the parking lot near the ferry.

The misty rain continued for most of the day. The rain was light, and most fishermen had taken off their rain gear. Holden had left her waterproof gear in the truck. She and Gayle crossed on the ferry and were checking fishermen on the other side. They walked downstream, checking stringer counts and licenses, enjoying the time together. It was seldom they were able to spend this time working alongside one another. As the day ended they returned to the parking lot and said good night.

They hadn't been gone long when the huge brown bear made an appearance at the fishing hole. He ignored the few fishermen on the riverbank and went directly to fishing. He'd caught his third fish when the young female came to the high bank to watch the river and look for a good fishing spot. She came down the high bank and stepped into the river alongside the big bear. He gave her a careful look and poked his head into the water to catch a fish and carry it to the shore where he put it on the ground in front of her. It must have been love, for she gave a short snarl and began to eat the fish.

An hour later, with the big bear doing most of the fishing, the two bears climbed the steep bank and walked together down the bear trail toward the trees.

On the flight back from Cooper Landing, Les Goddard piloted the airplane with Wilson giving him directions from the rear seat. He instructed the new pilot to fly up the Killey River as far as the land was flat, but they turned back before reaching the steep valley leading up the mountain and to several small lakes in the area. Les flew back to Kenai River and turned downstream to return to the Soldotna Airport where Les parked the Super Cub and climbed out of the cabin with Wilson following.

Once the plane was tied down and the tanks filled, Wilson offered him a ride back to the office where his personal vehicle was parked.

"I'm impressed with your flying skills considering your lack of hours in the air. You handle the aircraft well and I've seen you use good judgment in tight situations. When you finish the academy, I hope they assign you to this post," this was Wilson's ultimate compliment to Les.

"I appreciate that, Sarge. I like the work, especially now since I have my license to fly. And I like working with Holden and you."

"This doesn't mean I'm letting you off the hook about your education. I expect you to be diligent with your studies and finish your degree. The department will keep you on without a degree, but if you want to be anything besides a Trooper working the riverbanks, you need that degree."

"Don't worry, Sarge. I plan to keep up with my studies. Holden has given me this same message, by the way." Both men laughed.

Sergeant Wilson became more serious, "You've probably figured out that Holden is an exceptional officer. She never balks at an assignment and always does an outstanding job. If she tells you something, you really should listen."

They were entering the parking area at the office now, "OK, Sarge. I liked the flight, especially the trip back to town," said Les, chuckling. "And you don't have to worry, I plan to finish my degree, but in a slightly different major. I think I'll need some law classes and possibly a justice degree. I'm going to look into that. I want you to know I appreciate what you've done for me. I'll try to never let you down."

Wilson smiled as he entered the office building. He turned to wave at his new officer as he entered. 'This kid is going to be a good officer,' he thought to himself.

An hour and a half later Holden drove her State truck onto the parking lot. It had been an uneventful day of routine work. In the office she worked another hour on daily reports to leave for the Boss. She hoped the Sergeant would pull her off Russian River duty and let her go back to regular patrol. Hunting season wasn't far off, and she'd like to have fresh knowledge of the sideroads and tracts, noting any changes since last year.

She'd driven home, had her shower and was wondering if she should broil a burger on the grill, when her doorbell jingled. It was Les with a large bag in his hands.

"Hi, Holden. I thought I'd make dinner tonight. I hope you like Mama Mia Pizza and a glass of Cabernet," he said, holding up the large bag.

"You're just in time. I was about to fix something but didn't know what I wanted. Come on in, we can go to the back deck."

"You already know the Boss let me fly the Cub back to Soldotna. I can't tell you how good it is to find a job I really enjoy. I look forward to coming to work every day. A lot of that pleasure comes from you and your teaching me the ropes. I know we probably won't work together after I finish the Trooper Academy but thank you for

guiding me through these first months." He
poured two glasses of red wine and held one out to
her. He raised his own and toasted his partner.

She touched her glass to his and drank a sip.
"You're a good partner, Les. You've earned any
breaks you get. I've had temporary officers to
work with in the past and I must say you have been
the best I've ever had. I thank you." She raised her
glass to toast him. He touched her glass with his
and dug out the pizza.

CHAPTER 30

The light rains continued for the next several days, making it uncomfortable to walk the long distance from the ferry crossing to the bear's fishing hole. The crowds of sport fishermen had thinned and only a few were seen on the river banks. Betty Holden and Les Goddard were becoming very bored with so little to do and with so much time to get it done. They'd come to the fishing hole to watch for the big bear and sat on the same log for many days with no results. The bear they'd been watching was nowhere to be seen. The low ceilings and rain had kept aircraft searches out of the equation.

As they sat on the log, drinking hot coffee, they discussed duties they would face in the next few days of Goddard's summer hire contract. Les was looking forward to going to the Trooper Academy in the fall.

It was shortly after noon when Sergeant Wilson's phone rang. It was the supervisor at the Kenai Jail Facility. "Hello Ted," he said in a cheerful voice when the Sarge answered.

"Oh, hello Roy. How are things in the lock-up?" he asked.

"Just another day in paradise," he quipped. "I just called to let you know we looked at the phone records for your friend Donnigan. Most of his calls were made to his attorney, but he did make several calls to Anchorage to a number listed to Lou Phelps. I'll mark them and make you a copy. My transportation officer will be coming to Soldotna in about an hour. I'll have him deliver you a copy of the phone record."

"That sounds great, Roy. I'll be waiting to see it."

An hour later the jail officer dropped the envelope on Lynda Dorn's desk. She took it to Sergeant Wilson who began to study it as soon as he opened the envelope.

There were several calls from Donnigan to Phelps. All were made in late afternoon, usually around three o'clock. The calls were not evidence of wrongdoing, but to Wilson were suspicious and could indicate the men were conspiring to commit another crime.

Ted Wilson decided to call Walker, the DA. "Hello Walker," he greeted the lawyer, "I just got a copy of phone calls made by our friend Burt Donnigan and learned he's made several calls to Lou Phelps in Anchorage. They may just be idle chit chat, but I think he may be attempting to get Phelps to get the big brown bear for him. I know this is a reach, but Burt is obsessed enough to do that sort of thing. I guess the reason I called you about this is that I don't know what to do about it. Have you got any ideas?"

There was a long pause, "I don't have any ideas for you Ted. Your information is worth noting, but we have no real grounds to contact him about it. He has his rights too, you know."

"Yeah, I know. But it's my job to protect wildlife from men like him and Burt. I don't have enough manpower to assign someone to do nothing but to watch out for someone going fishing with a rifle."

"Sorry I couldn't be more help, Ted. I get frustrated from time to time, too. If you think of a way to take care of the problem, just give me a call and let me know."

"OK, Walker. I'll do that." Wilson hung up the phone, leaned back in his chair, took off his cap and rubbed the back of his neck. He uttered a huge sigh and tossed the sheet of phone numbers into his 'In' basket.

Sergeant Ted Wilson was still in his office when Holden and Goddard returned to the parking lot. Holden went inside to do her daily report. Les went inside to leave some gear in his locker.

Wilson heard them enter and asked them to come to his office for a few minutes.

"Hi, Sarge, you're here late today," said Holden.

"Yeah, I wanted to see you two before I quit today. How was your day on the river?"

"Quiet, very quiet," said Betty.

"Did you see any bears today?" asked Wilson.

"One small brown bear and one black bear that was just passing by on the river trail. There aren't many fish in the river now."

"Hunting season opens in a short couple of weeks and this rain is set to continue for several more days. I'm going to have you and Les patrol Mystery Creek Road all the way out the pipeline. Hunters are going to be setting up camps out there and I don't want any early birds getting an early moose. Stay visible and let them know we're in the area. Old Les here, only has a few more days to work and we don't want him to catch a cold out there in the open with the rain coming down like it is." Wilson again took off his cap and rubbed his head.

"Thanks, Sarge, I've been worried about that. He's kinda delicate, you know," offered Holden.

"If you two keep on talking that way I think I'll call someone to report child abuse," it was Les' turn to tease.

Wilson was smiling now, "On the serious side, I want you two to know I'm very proud of the job you've done up at the Russian River. Gayle has mentioned to me several times what a great help you two have been to her these past weeks."

"Have you given any more thought to Burt's hunting partners and what they may be up to?" asked Holden.

"Yes. And I can't think of anything we can do. I talked with DA Walker and he couldn't give me any help with what to do about it. But I have an idea. I think I'll have an Anchorage FWP officer contact Lou Phelps to let him know we are keeping an eye on him. Hopefully, that'll be enough to keep him from going after the bear. The DA doesn't feel good about us violating his or Burt's civil rights."

"I hope that works, Boss," said Betty. "I'm going to my office and finish my daily report." She turned to Les, "I'll see you at 0700 and we can go for a nice drive down the pipeline road."

The following morning, shortly after Les and Betty had driven away from the office, Ted Wilson called his counterpart in the Anchorage office. "Hello, Ed," Ted greeted the answering voice.

"Hi there, Ted. What's up?" he asked.

I have a small dilemma down here, Ed." Wilson went on to explain the problem and asked his friend to send an officer to speak with Phelps. "We don't need to make any threats, just let him know he's under the microscope. I'm hoping it'll spook him enough to keep him away from the big bear for a while. The animal should be leaving the river soon and be returning to the mountain for the winter. Burt Donnigan is scheduled for a court hearing in a week. He's been denied bail because he violated his conditions of release last time he bailed out. The DA said he believes Burt will get a long jail sentence for this one. I hope he's right."

"OK Ted, I'll see what I can do for you and get back with the results."

Satisfied he had done all he could do Wilson turned his attention to the mundane duties of managing the Fish and Wildlife Post.

The trip up Mystery Creek Road was all new for Les. He had never been up this road except for the one short trip to rescue a hiker. The scenery was beautiful. The pipeline road was rough and in bad repair which made for very slow going. One bridge was so bad Holden decided to ford the stream rather than chance crossing it. They spotted several cow moose, some with calves, as they drove up the single-track road. The two airstrips on the road were also in poor condition, but an aircraft on tundra tires, those huge, under inflated tires were three feet tall and over a foot wide and could easily land and take off on both of these weedy airstrips.

There were many Spruce hens pecking gravel along the roadway. "Are they really good to eat?" asked Les.

"Yes, in the fall when they're eating berries. You know, elderberries and wild cranberries and such. In the winter they eat a lot of spruce needles and buds. They get awfully strong tasting then," she answered.

As they came to the small stream called Chickaloon Creek, near the end of the third airstrip, the king salmon were spawning in the stream. A small brown bear, probably a three-year-old, was fishing for the big salmon. Betty stopped the truck to watch the bear stand in the shallow stream waiting for a big salmon to get within reach. It took only a few minutes, and he had a fish, which appeared to be somewhere in the neighborhood of twenty pounds. He carried the fish to the dry roadway and laid down to eat it.

"Now, there's a sight you don't see in downtown Milwaukee," said Holden.

Les chuckled, "You know?" he said, "I think I'm the luckiest guy in the world. Working with you, I've seen things most folks never get to see. Watching this bear is one of them. The average person would never be able to see this except on TV on the National Geographic Channel. I'm going to miss working with you, Holden. I thank you for giving me the opportunity to enjoy these things."

The two officers sat at the site and watched the bear for nearly an hour before he walked into the trees upstream from the crossing. Holden drove through the water and up the road past the last airstrip and on to where a hiking trail went up the mountain.

"We're almost to the end of the road, Les. There's a side road that goes down off the side. Back a few miles, there's an old road behind the other airstrip. It goes down to the Chickaloon Flats. Duck hunters like to go down there to hunt. The road is getting very overgrown, and it can knock the mirrors off your truck. I'm not going down there today, but there's an old hunting cabin down there. Two old guys had the place and kept horses and chickens. I was told their names were the "Two Jims". They've been gone a long time, of course, but the last time I was down there it was still a usable cabin."

"I don't know how much longer I'll be able to work with you Betty, but I thank you for what you've taught me. I hope I can be as good an officer as you are." he looked down at his feet.

"Let's get back to the office, Partner," she said with a smile.

Over the next several days the huge brown bear left his mate behind and was moving down the river toward Skilak Lake. He had gained nearly two hundred pounds of pure fat that would keep him nourished during the coming winter. Once he reached the lake, he walked up the glacier fed stream to the left of the lake and crossed to the wooded hillsides below the glacier. The days were becoming shorter, and he wanted to rest a large part of the day. The big grizzly made his way up the sidehills to a spot below the glacier to a place he had been before. It was where he had once killed a large horse and buried it before consuming all of it earlier this year.

He continued up the hillside to find a spot to dig a shallow depression and line the bottom with grass and twigs. The snow would come soon, and he wanted to be ready. He wasn't eating much now, only cleaning his system for the long sleep ahead. The snow and wind would cover him for the winter, and no one would be able to see him sleeping through the dark winter days. Life was good for this giant of the Kenai Peninsula.